Heritage

MICHELLE DOREY

DEDICATION

To my readers. I'm forever grateful.

CONTENTS

ONE

I t's not my fault you know!" It was late and I was on edge
from Gwen's bitching. "I can't help it that the last two
places were a bust!" I looked over at her and rolled my
eyes. On six hours of sleep and an empty stomach, there were
so many other places I'd rather be.

Gwen's fingers raked through her hair and she huffed
sharply. "The crazy old woman in Maine wasn't bad enough?
She was *psychotic* not psychic! Then we go to Whispering
Willows? That was a treat! A harebrained scheme to promote a
haunted bed and breakfast, hoping we'd lend credibility to it?"
She glared over at me for a split second before turning her eyes
back to the road. "Which, by the way, *wasn't* haunted."

"I know, I know!" I took a deep breath, but even so, it
wasn't enough to keep from lashing out. "Maybe if you'd done
more *research* on them, we could have been spared the
inconvenience."

Gwen looked at me for a long second. "That's Thompson's
job, isn't it?"

I pointed straight ahead. "Watch the road, will ya!" A thick
fog was rolling in over the winding highway. To make matters
worse, every mile or so there was a sign warning of a moose
magically popping out to attack us. A moose, not a deer. A.
Freaking. Moose. I'd never seen a moose in real life, but I'm

pretty sure they're bigger than any deer. And deer are big enough. "Last thing we need is to hit Bullwinkle out here in the middle of nowhere!"

Gwen turned her attention back to her driving, but it didn't stop her from snapping back at me. "Research! I thought Mr. Thompson was supposed to do screening, to weed out the phony claims. What the hell are you paying him for?"

She had a point, and this discussion was getting out of hand. I sighed. "Yeah. I'll have a talk with him when we get back."

"Glad to hear it," she muttered. "Won't get us out of this one though." She shook her head. "I mean, honestly, Keira; how did your grandmother do it? Surely, she didn't travel the world, chasing bogus hauntings and manifestations for all those years."

I rested my forehead in my hand. "I don't know. She didn't stick around long enough to tell me all the details, you know."

"Yeah... I guess so. You only knew her for what—two weeks before she passed on?" She glanced at me from the corner of her eye just for a second.

I snorted. "Yeah, *that's* the term, *passed on*... she was already dead when I met her."

"When *I met* her too, y'know. I met her twice and she looked, acted and felt like a regular flesh and blood person. I was blown away when we learned she had been dead for weeks!" Gwen shook her head and added in a voice filled with wonder, "That's why I signed on for this crazy job."

We both went silent for a few minutes thinking back over those few days in the strangest summer of our lives. In the span of less than two weeks my parents had banished me to my grandmother's—a woman I didn't even know existed—to become some sort of half-assed exorcist of ghosts. 'Cuz, you know, if I didn't, the world would end. How many 23 year olds get to save the universe?

Oh, and the Nana I met and grew to love dearly in that *waaay* too short span of time was already dead herself. She had hung out on this plane of existence just long enough to rope me into this vocation, and without even so much as a kiss goodbye or a poof of smoke, just disappeared over to the other side.

I barely had enough time to get to know her; yet the connection we forged in those short days left a hole in my heart. I sighed. "Yeah, there's a lot she didn't tell me."

"I'm tired of the running around for nothing, Keira. I just want to sleep in my own bed. It's been almost two weeks now."

"Oh come on! We've travelled first class—hell, *better* than first class all the way! Chartered jets? Five star hotels? Not to mention the shopping in Boston!"

She shrugged. "That's more your style than mine. I was just a simple letter carrier, still living at home with my father out in the boonies when this whole thing started." She arched an eyebrow but kept her eyes on the road. "You're the one with the New York City la-ti-dah background, not me."

I waved my hands in surrender. "Look, if this one's a fraud too, we'll take some time off. Maybe we need to be more discerning about which cases we choose to work on. It wouldn't hurt to tune Mr. Thompson up either. His office should do more in screening."

"Good." That was pretty curt.

"Fine." I could be curt too and crossed my arms. My grandmother had made it her life's work to transition spirits to the other realm. And now, I, or rather my cranky *partner and I*, were carrying on with this. Nana had never warned me of the false hits I was bound to come across.

I sat up straight seeing the small sign at the side of the road—'Bolly's Bay' I pointed at the sign. "We're here." Which really didn't mean very much. After the sign announcing our arrival in the hamlet, there were just a few houses. "Where do we meet this guy?"

Gwen shook her head as she slowed the car. "And for your information, *I did* do some research on this one. The guy's name is Stanley Hartley. He's 38 years old and has been married fourteen years. Two kids, a daughter 13 and a son who's 10. His wife's named Maggie. Currently, they've been holed up in a neighbor's home for the last week. Their daughter was flung down the stairs by an unseen force. That episode was the last of a series that hit this family from the day they moved in."

I stared at her. "Oh?"

"Yeah, 'Oh'. I did my own *research* on this case after the idiocy we dealt with back in Maine."

"Oh."

"Yeah. 'Oh'. Right. The daughter's fine, by the way—a mild sprain and a bump on the head." She fluttered her fingers on the steering wheel. "I've been emailing Stan back and forth the last two days."

I stifled a yawn. "A family of four living in someone's living room or something? That must be great for their neighbors."

"Keira." Gwen breathed sharply through her nose. "This is Newfoundland."

"What's that supposed to mean?" She was looking at me like I did something wrong.

"It's the way it is out here is what. Maybe people don't get involved back in New York like that, but out here, neighbors look out for each other, okay?"

Gwen was only three years older than me, but I got to tell you, sometimes she made me feel like a stupid kid. I shrugged. "Yeah, whatever." I shrugged again. "At least that's what he *said* happened. We've had people blow smoke at us the last two times, right?"

"It wouldn't kill you to help with that. You can find out real quick if he's full of it; all you got to do is shake his hand."

"It comes and goes, Gwen. Sometimes I see what they're thinking like that," I snapped my fingers. "But then other times I don't get anything." It was one of the few gifts that blossomed in me when I first showed up at my Nana's doorstep. But it wasn't reliable.

"How about you concentrate on getting a read on him when we meet him? Just *try* Keira. Can you at least do that?" She pointed with her chin up ahead. "There's the gas station

4

we're supposed to meet him at." She pulled the car into the parking area and fished out her phone. She punched a number and held the phone to her ear. Still looking at me, she added, "Wouldn't hurt you to try."

"Okay! Okay!"

Gwen spoke into her phone, and ended the call. "He'll be here in just a few minutes and take us up to the place."

"Alright." I nestled into my seat. "I'm going to try to clear my mind then." I hadn't done this exercise since I was with Nana months ago. When she first showed me I had the gift, she taught me how to clear my mind. I did a deep breathing exercise and relaxed into the quiet, with my eyes closed.

The glare of a set of headlights caused me to open my eyes. I kept my mind as clear as I could as I watched Stan get out of his pickup truck and come over to Gwen's side of the car. Stan. Not Stanley—he hated the formal version of his name.

My eyes grew wider, but I didn't say a word. Wow. I still had it. Big-time! I gave my head a small shake and relaxed again, clearing my mind.

He was tall and wearing a well worn parka. Despite the fact that he was only 38, his weathered face was a map of worry lines.

"Hi. I'm Stan Hartley." He pushed his rough hand through the gaping window at Gwen.

Shaking his hand, she said, "Hi. I'm Gwen," She glanced over at me and then back to him. "This is Keira Swanson. She's the one in charge."

My eyes flickered to Gwen before I leaned over past her to shake the guy's hand. "Actually, we're more of a team. How's your daughter's ankle?"

Stan's arms spread on the hood of the car and he leaned over, his face filling the window. "She's hobblin' around but at least it didn't break." His eyes closed for a moment and then he sighed. "At first I didn't believe them about the house being haunted. I blame myself for her gettin' hurt. And she's not the only one. My son, Robert is afraid to go to sleep. He's having terrible nightmares and such. The Missus, she's hardly said a word to me since Emily was hurt."

"I'm so sorry. We'll see about—"

"I never should have bought the place. We left everything to come here...get back to the land and all with the farmin'. I'm all beat out from working the fishin' boats since I was a lad." He shook his head with slow sorrow. "I was warned. But not until after the offer to buy the house had been accepted and we couldn't back out...not that I would have, you understand. I didn't know then, what I know now. That place is bad. Why else would it have been vacant for so many years?" Stan's eyes began to water and his hand swept over his face to clear them. "I'm at my wit's end. You got to help us."

Gwen cleared her throat and looked down at the steering wheel. "We'll do what we can." I could tell that she was sceptical, and I didn't blame her.

Except Stan was telling the truth, plain and simple. A picture had flashed in my mind when I shook his hand, the fights with his wife, the children crying and being scared out of their minds, huddled in their beds. Even though I'd only touched him for a second, it had all come pouring into my mind.

I cleared my throat. "Take us to the house. We'll follow right behind you in the car."

"Right now?" his eyes widened with wonder. "Pretty late, y'know."

"No time like the present," I said, ignoring the surprised look Gwen shot me.

"Right away, ma'am!" Stan pivoted and ran to his truck.

"This one's for real, Gwen," I said as she started the car and followed him. "I saw the whole thing when we shook hands."

"Okay. Well, here goes nothing," she said.

She couldn't have been more wrong.

TWO

It seemed to take forever creeping down the long lane after we turned off the main road. The fog was watered milk, obscuring all but the red tail lights of Stan's car as we drove along the gravel drive. When his brake lights lit up, a two storey clapboard house loomed like a dark sentinel.

"Honey, we're home!" I flashed a limp smile at Gwen, trying not to think of the tangled knot sinking low in my gut. Seeing her scowl, I shrugged. "What? It's a joke. Lighten up."

She shot me a dirty look. "You said this one's for real, right?" When I nodded, I saw her face cloud with fear. "I've seen 'for real' with you before, Keira." She glanced over at Stan, waiting next to his truck. "Fake ones are a pain, yeah... but 'for real'..." she shuddered.

I put a hand on her shoulder. Fear bordering on terror shot through me from Gwen's heart. I couldn't blame her. The only two times she had encountered spirits, there'd been demons involved. It was scary as hell and dangerous. For both of us. "Hey!" I said, my voice bright. "Just another day at the office, no biggie!"

She sighed and got out of the car, pulling her suede coat closed around her.

I stepped out of the car into the darkening, bone chilling evening. The fog slithered over the headlights of the car. I shoved my hands in the deep pockets of my down coat and my fingers closed around the black tourmaline stone that my grandmother had given me. I could almost see Nana's dark blue eyes spark and hear her words, *'tourmaline is the strongest protection stone against psychic attack'*. I might not need it for this house but just in case...

Stan's head jerked to the side indicating the small stoop and steps leading up to the house. "The door is open. It's too bad someone hadn't burglar'd the bugger and burned it to the ground. That way I'd get the insurance money. As it is, I've sunk all I have in it." He let out a sigh as he eyed the two of us up and down. "If this don't work, I'm done for..."

Gwen's hand rose to rest on his shoulder. God! She was only a little shorter than his six feet hulk. "I'll call you when we're done here. Go back to your family, Stan," she said.

Immediately a look of relief crossed his face. "You're sure you don't need me?" He was already shuffling over to his truck.

"We've got this. Gwen's right." In no time he was off down the lane, his tires throwing up chunks of gravel. I gazed at the house, the dark windows on the second floor like eyes peering down at me. I took a deep breath and turned to Gwen. "Ready?"

She nodded and plucked her cell phone from her pocket, turning the flashlight app on. Slowly, she led the way up the steps, her boots sounding sharp against the groaning wood. The fog swirled over my shoulders and I shivered, waiting for her to push the door open.

The beam of her phone caught a long hallway next to a set of worn stairs before shining on the wall next to us. The hair on the back of my neck rose high, tingling even before spotting the light switch and flipping it on. We weren't alone.

A thud from the right and my heart sprang into my throat.

The room where it had come from was deep in shadow with a slice of light piercing the arched entry, revealing a sofa and coffee table. As I stared into the room, a greyish form took shape, gliding quickly towards us.

"Watch out!" I stepped in front of Gwen, shielding her.

She angled her head past me gazing around but not seeing the ghost. "There's something here, isn't there? It's icy cold in here."

"Oh yeah. It's right in front of me."

Gwen gasped, but I ignored her; the apparition in front of me had my complete attention. I stiffened when features began to appear on it. It was an old man, his dark eyes hard as stone while his mouth was twisted in an angry snarl. I gasped myself when its fingers gripped my arm with an almost electric jolt that fired right up into my chest. There was a sharp pain like a knife in my lungs, making it hard to breathe.

Horace. His name pulsed in my head.

"You don't belong here." I managed to get the words out, yanking my arm away.

The sofa slammed over backwards, and the low coffee table shot like a bullet across the room. I jerked back and Gwen's fingers closed over my forearm.

"Oh my God, Keira! This is for real!" Her hand slid down my arm and gripped mine. It was just like the time in her house with the Ouija board and then in my grandmother's room. Whatever power we each had, when we joined hands, it became magnified, a quadrillion times stronger. My heart slowed and I took a deep breath, watching the entity falter. There was a pulse and it faded, becoming transparent.

"Horace, it is time for you to go." I stood straighter, squeezing Gwen's hand for all I was worth. My other hand rose like a traffic cop, extended to the wispy trails that the ghost had vaporized into. This was a man who had lived in the house all his life. There was fear in his essence. Fear of letting go. Confusion. And anger. A lot of anger. But not at me. But then at who?

I gasped at the sounds of a series of thuds descended the

stairs. A striped rubber ball bounced on each step and then rolled over to rest next to the toe of my boot.

"Oh my God..." Gwen's voice was soft and my eyes followed her gaze to the top of the stairs.

The ball bouncing down the stairs reminded me of another child ghost I had met last summer. His name had been Sam; a sweet, poor tortured soul. But not this time. At the head of the stairs the misty shape of another young boy shimmered. His eyes glowed red above a dark gaping yawn of a mouth. Where Sam had been a woeful waif, this kid was pure malevolence.

And he wasn't alone. A woman in a long, dark dress drifted over to stand behind him. Small orbs of light, dozens of them, meandered down the stairs coming towards us! How the hell many of these things were *in* this house? Gwen and I were seriously outnumbered!

The overhead light flashed bright and then exploded. Glass tinkled to the floor leaving us in total darkness. Gwen's hand tugged at mine.

"Keira! Let's get out of here!" She jerked me towards the door that still stood open.

"No, Gwen! We can do this. Get your light." It was all a tactic to get us to leave. They were bringing out the big guns, but we could do it!

"No freaking way! C'mon!" She almost picked me up; she was pulling so hard to get me out of there.

"What the hell are you doing?" I struggled against her.

"I'm doing what I was told to do! I'm your Guardian, and this is dangerous!"

Guardian. Yeah. "Okay!" I turned and she hustled me out the door.

Our feet no sooner hit the front stoop when the door whooshed shut with such force that it shook the wood under our feet. I stumbled down the steps but Gwen's grip kept me aloft, racing to the car.

When we were inside she gulped and stared at the house. "We've got to be better prepared if we're going to do this. Stan and his family were lucky to escape." She leaned forward in her seat to stare at the house. "I actually saw something at the top of the stairs! I couldn't make it out, but I saw it!"

"Did you see the ball?"

"What ball?"

I shuddered. Definitely demons inside. They were able to sense *my* memory of Sam and tossed the ball to catch me off guard. Worked like a charm, too.

I peered at the house, trying desperately to catch my breath. What would Nana have done in this situation? For the life of me, I didn't know. It had been too short a time with her.

I turned to Gwen, "Sure, there are lots of entities in there, and it might take a few days, but we can do it. We just need to tackle them one at a time. The thing in Nana's bedroom had been ten times as bad and we beat it back." Even to my own ears, it sounded like false bravado.

"Sure, Keira. We'll just march back in there and say shoo. How'd that work out the first time?" Her hands shook as she reached for the key to get the car going again. "We weren't ready for that. We go from two false alarms to *Hell House*." She sighed as she backed the car up and turned the wheel. "It's making my job at the post office look better and better, let me tell you."

"Give me your phone."

She scowled at me and threaded the car along the misty lane. "What's wrong with yours?"

"You've got Stan's number captured on yours. We need to see him and make some kind of arrangements for the night." I took the phone she extended and pushed the button to call up his number.

"We're seriously going to do this, huh?"

She was plucking the tautness of my last nerve and I had to work to keep my voice calm. "What do you mean? Of course we are! Think about their kids. The house is all that family has and it was their dream home!" I pointed a finger at her accusingly. "This is what we do! You know as well as I, that these ghosts have to go. If we don't do it, who will?" I held the phone to my ear.

"That was quick!" Stan's voice drilled into my eardrum.

"Hi. It's not done yet. We need to tackle it again. But first, where can we find food and a bed for the night?" Now that we were out of the house, the dread and fear of what we'd been through hit me with a wallop. I'd been tired before but now, my body was trembling. I leaned over and yanked the heat knob all the way up.

"If you're looking for a hotel, there aren't any...not for sixty miles anyway." There was a pause and I could hear his muffled voice speaking to someone else in the background. After a few moments he came back on, "You can stay at my friend's mother's house. You two will have to share a bed but, she's got a spare room."

I looked over at Gwen. She was going to just love this—NOT! "Where is it? Actually, where are you?" The woman probably had a sofa. I'd bed down there and give Gwen the room. With her height, it would probably work out better.

"It's easier if I just meet you at the gas station again. I'd like to talk to you, private like. See you in five minutes." There was a click and I handed the phone back to my partner. "He's found us a place for the night...at his friend's mother's place. Maybe she'll take pity on us and give us a slice of toast or something."

"This is sure a glamorous job, Keira. You could buy and sell this whole village and here we are begging a room. How did your grandmother manage this?"

It was a good question.

THREE

The old woman set a bowl of soup and homemade buns in front of me. The heat and aroma from her wood cook stove mingled with the smell of the food and I felt the nervousness evaporate from my chest.

Gwen picked up the golden roll and began breaking it into smaller pieces. "This is awfully nice of you, Mrs. Kirkpatrick, to let us stay the night. The soup smells wonderful."

The old woman's face broke into a wide smile as she took a seat across from us. Her gnarled hands folded together in front of her and she leaned in, "T'is not much. If I'd known I'd have ye girls here, I'd made something worthwhile. T'is naught but a drop of soup to give ye."

I had never heard such an accent before in my life and I found it charming as hell. I took a spoonful of soup and my eyebrows rose high. You'd pay an arm and a leg for a soup like that in Gramercy Tavern in New York. "It's delicious. I'd really like to give you some money for putting us up like this."

"Don't be insultin' me wit dat. Sure, it's been too long since I had anyone to cook for." Her pale blue eyes narrowed. "I could have told ye about dat house, if anyone had bothered to ask. It's an abomination, is what it is. Saints alive, that poor family to spend good money on the likes of it!" She shook her head and tsked a few times.

Gwen's eyes sparked to life and she swallowed quickly. "So you've lived in Bolly's Bay all your life? What's the story on the house?"

Mrs. Kirkpatrick's gaze went skyward and her hand fluttered making the sign of the cross over her forehead and shoulders. "It was old Captain Smythe who had the house built back in the eighteen hundreds. You cain't see it at this time of night, and in this pea soup fog, but it sits on a jut of land, overlookin' the sea. He raised his family there but the children took off as soon as they were old enough. The next crew who lived there were an odd bit of goods." She nodded and her eyes flared wide, as if we were supposed to know exactly what an 'odd bit of goods' was.

"How so? What did they do that was so strange?"

"They kept to themselves, they did. Would hardly speak if they weren't asked to. They used to have big bonfires that lasted well into the night. Talk was, t'were witches. I was just a twinkle in me Dad's eye, but I remember the talk for years after. The whole family found dead by the constabulary. Poisoned." Her mouth pursed and she looked over at our bowls. "Would you care for another bit of soup?"

Witches. A family of them. It would explain all the entities that we'd seen. It would also explain why we'd failed to rouse them out of the house and why they were so hostile.

"No thanks. The soup was great. It hit the spot." Gwen placed her spoon in the bowl and rose to her feet to take it to the sink. She turned and leaned against the counter, gazing at the old woman. "So after they lived there, it's been empty ever since?"

"I wish it were so. No. A few families tried to settle there but they never stayed long. And now...poor Stan. I could have told him, if he'd asked. But no. Fresh from the big city, knowing everything there was to know about life. He thought it was going to be simple...but there's nothing simple about the Smythe home."

"Have you ever been in it, Mrs. Kirkpatrick?" I stifled a yawn. I was ready for bed, to get some time alone to cipher this out, but the old lady looked like she was just getting warmed up.

"Only once, on a dare. Three of us went there one Halloween night. Only two of us left that horrid place." Her eyes glazed over as she stared down at the lace table cloth. "Mike Feeney was never the sharpest knife in the drawer. He was puttin' on airs, acting all brave to impress me older sister, Maeve. He pranced up the stairs and that was the last time we saw him. Gone, vanished right out of thin air."

"Did they search for him? He couldn't have just disappeared." Gwen pushed off from the counter and took a seat again.

"Aye! The place were searched. I tell ye, he just disappeared. "Her fingers thrummed on the table. "And now, the two of ye, thinkin' ye can fix it. Best to clear out of Bolly's Bay and forget you ever saw the Smythe house. Mark my words...nothin' good will come of it."

I shook my head and my gaze dropped. She meant well but we couldn't do that. "We appreciate your concern but we've got to give it one more shot."

Gwen cleared her throat and then stood up. "We hate to break this up after you being so kind to us, but I've got to get some rest."

Mrs. Kirkpatrick folded her hands together and sighed. I took the opportunity to clear my dishes. But she wasn't letting us go without the final word.

"Ye'll be in my prayers," she said, her mouth downcast and silent for only a moment. Lifting her face to me, she continued, "Now, are you sure you want to sleep down on the sofa? The bed's a double with plenty of room, even if this one here's a lanky colt." She nodded her head towards Gwen.

"No. I'll be fine down here. I'll just go up and wash my face before I settle in for the night. Thanks again, Mrs.

Kirkpatrick." Gwen and I left the over-sized country kitchen, grabbed our overnight bags from the foyer, and went up the stairs. I followed her in the small bedroom and plunked myself down on the soft bed.

"What do you think?" I looked up at her while she took a seat next to me.

She sat with a sigh. "Let me get this straight. We're here to deal with ghosts, and we've had to cope with demons back at your grandmother's." She turned to me, her mouth hanging open. "Now *witches*? What's next? Zombies?"

"Do you know anything about how to get rid of witches?" I asked.

"What? Nooo! And I take it your grandmother didn't cover that part." Dark cusps were under Gwen's eyes and the freckles on her nose looked more pronounced in her pale face. She was so tired.

I slapped my thighs. "Witches or not, they're ghosts and have to transition. This crew's got to go, one way or another." Yawning myself now, I rose to my feet. "We've got to get some sleep. It'll be better in the morning. See you then."

Ten minutes later I entered the living room where Mrs. Kirkpatrick had left a blanket and pillow on the sofa. But that wasn't all. I picked up the loop of pearly beads while the cross affixed to it swung back and forth. Even though I wasn't a Catholic, I knew it was a rosary. I also figured that Mrs. Kirkpatrick probably had a priest in the church, bless it with holy water.

A sense of peace filled me as I snuggled in under the homemade quilt. The old woman was doing her part to help us with the most powerful ammunition in her world. At this point, I would take whatever assistance was offered.

FOUR

The next day, when we left the house, our bellies full and bodies rested, the sun was high in a cloudless sky. Gwen's hand fell over my arm and she grinned staring along the street. Word had got round about the two young women trying to clear the Smythe house of the evil spirits. Young and old meandered along the sidewalks, or stood at the edge of their front yards, casting curious stares at us.

Stan hurried forward, dragging a red haired woman in a plaid wool jacket by the arm. When they stopped, he tugged her forward. "Maggie, these are the two girls."

She shook his hand away and her chin rose high, staring at us with grey, narrow eyes. "You look pretty young to be at this kind of thing."

I extended my hand to her and when our fingers touched, a flash of her fear threaded through me. But not for her own sake; it was more for her children, and the dire financial straits of moving back to the city after abandoning the house. There was also an old woman, her mother, pleased as punch that she'd been proven right in her admonition for them to stay in the city. "Pleased to meet you, Maggie. I'm Keira and this is my partner, Gwen."

Maggie nodded and reached for Gwen's hand. As she did, I piped up. "Your mother...Maureen, she's wrong. We'll fix this problem, Maggie, and your children will be fine."

Her eyes flew open wide just for a second, then she looked over at her husband. "You've got a big mouth!" she snapped at him.

I still held Maggie's hand. "Stan didn't tell me anything. Like he never told me how he always disliked being called Stanley." Now I had both their attention. I turned to Stan. "And nobody told me about how Maggie's mother never felt you were good enough for her, Stan."

"How did you know?" She turned to glance at her husband. "You must have—"

"No. He never said anything about your mother, just your children." I placed my hand on her arm and stepped to the side for Gwen to carry the bags to the car. Maggie was totally gobsmacked by what I just did.

"No! You..."

I put my arm around her and we stepped aside. I leaned into her ear. "The first boy to kiss you was named Kyle, and it was in the first grade. You thought he was gross, but you also felt special."

She sucked in her mouth and stared at me silently. I felt fear begin to well up in her. Uh oh—I had pushed it too far. I patted her shoulder. "Take it easy, Maggie, Gwen and I are the good guys." I felt her fear abate and chided myself for showing off. "Look, last night, we weren't prepared for what met us. Today, we are."

I left her open mouthed, walking quickly along the walkway to join Gwen in the car. The smile on Gwen's face as she drove along the street, doing the regal wave to the entire village it seemed, made me laugh.

Her eyebrow cocked high and she flashed a grin at me. "Show off."

"Hey! It was just a little mind reading, that's all. It's not like I levitated the luggage or anything! That would have really freaked them out."

"You didn't think that maybe, it might have helped *me*? You could have whooshed the luggage with a nod, but instead I'm carting it like some kind of pack horse." She shook her head and tsked loudly.

I wasn't about to tell her that I was still having trouble with telekinesis. More often than not when I practised moving simple objects even, like a glass of water, it was as likely to fly off the table and smash as move even a few inches.

"Here we go again." Gwen leaned forward peering out the windshield at the turn off from the main road.

As we drove down the lane, I sat straighter, squaring my shoulders, especially when the old house came into view. The old lady had been right. It was on a jut of land, surrounded on three sides by the water. There was a large outbuilding with snow still clinging to the shadowed areas. The house was in need of paint and a few of the shutters were askew, victims of the elements within and without.

Gwen parked the car in front of the small weathered stoop and turned to me. "Let's not rush into this. I think it's important to ground ourselves, calm our fear before we go in there."

"Agreed." I reached in my pocket and withdrew the rosary that Mrs. Kirkpatrick had given me. "I have my amulet...the stone that Nana gave me. I think you should carry this."

Her fingers closed over the rosary so only the crucifix was resting on her thumb. She nodded and slipped it in her pocket, settling deeper into the seat and taking measured breaths.

My eyes closed and I inhaled a long breath and held it. I repeated it three more times. *Nana, if you're anywhere around, help us with this.* Whether it was the breathing exercise or my silent prayer, I felt a calm strength fill my chest. We were here to do what was right. What we'd be dealing with inside were spirits. It didn't matter that they were witches in real life. They died proving that whatever malevolent power they had faith in, betrayed them. It was time for them to move on and leave the living in the peace they were entitled to.

I opened my eyes and looked over at Gwen. Her eyes were like steel, staring back at me. "Let's do this."

This time, when we went up the steps and pushed the door

open, our hands were joined. The power flowing between us was compelling; our joined hands made us as resolute as steel encased granite.

Entering the house, I felt the change as soon as we crossed the threshold. The air was heavy and I smelled decay. The hair on my arms and neck tingled and the space became icy cold. I glanced through the living room arch, but the spectre that was there last night was nowhere to be seen.

I squeezed Gwen's hand and then my voice boomed in the still air. I could feel it thunder in my throat. "I command you, with the power of light and life...show yourselves." I could hear Gwen's breathing beside me; see the dust motes drifting in the air highlighted by the sun filtering in the windows. My own heart beat a steady drum in my ears.

Taking another breath, I bellowed, "I COMMAND YOU! SHOW YOURSELVES NOW!"

My eyes opened wide as the boy materialized at the top of the stairs. The ball he'd tossed last night, started to bounce from the top step. My jaw set and feeling a force flow through me, focused on the small object. It stopped in mid-air. I lowered it down to the bottom of the staircase and rested it against the wall.

The woman in the long dress came into view, her black eyes glaring down at me. The orbs that had drifted above the stairs the night before, once more began their slow flight. My free hand slipped inside my coat pocket and closed tightly around the tourmaline stone. Another surge of white power flowed through my body, joined and magnified when Gwen held the rosary aloft.

The orbs stopped halfway down the stairs. They still hovered, but I *felt* their hesitation. And in that moment, the fear and confusion they were trying to instill in Gwen and I bounced back to them. *They* were afraid now. *That's right guys, I'm a different kind of cat.* Even the woman at the top landing shrank back.

Stepping forward, my voice was clear and loud, "Whoever you were in life, you are dead now. There is no place for you in this house." A shimmering blanket of energy radiated from my body, pushing forward towards the stairs.

"BEGONE! NOW!" Gwen's voice joined mine, the two of us striding forward, the silver wall of light expanding before us.

The boy's spectral image became blurred, his face morphing and then fading to nothing. The woman began to shrink and fade before she disappeared as well. There was only the dozen or so orbs of light above the steps. One by one, like bubbles from a child's soap wand, they popped when the wave of pure energy touched them.

They were gone. And with their departure so had the sense of rotting decay. The oppressive atmosphere lightened.

But it was still icy cold. The hair on my arms, even under my coat was still standing straight up.

It was then that the old man, the one who had rushed us the night before, materialized on the bottom stair. The wavering energy field swirled around his feet but did nothing to stop him from stepping closer. Gwen gasped and squeezed my hand hard enough to hurt.

I held the tourmaline stone before me. Still, the spectre approached, slow and steady, his ragged features becoming clearer and clearer. The muscle in my jaw clenched and then my words were low, "Who are you?" This spirit was nothing like the others had been; there was no sense of evil about him.

But he *was* consumed by fury.

"This is my house! Who are you?" His words filled my head and I glanced over at Gwen. Yeah, she saw him too. Her grey eyes were rimmed by the whites of them.

Realization flashed in my mind. "You're Captain Smythe." My heart was hammering in my chest like a piston but I didn't dare hesitate. "It's time for you to move on Captain, your watch is ended. But first, where is Mike Feeney? He was killed here and his body was never found."

The old spirit's form flickered and became dimmer. "He's gone. His body is in the sea. They tore him from limb to limb and threw the parts into the ocean. I tried but I couldn't save him! They were too many and too powerful!" He slowly turned

21

his head gazing around us before looking back to me. "But they be gone now, eh?"

"Yes. They're gone."

"Ta burn in hell?"

"I don't know. They're where they belong, I can assure you."

His mouth set. "Fair enough. Unearthly beasts, all of 'em." A small smile appeared on his face. "Thank you for ridding my home of these things...these evil beasts."

I nodded, and Gwen spoke up, her voice gentle. "Captain Smythe, it is time for you to leave, too."

It was enough to get me focussed again. Gwen was my strength and partner for a reason. I slid my hand from hers and stepped forward, extending it to the old soul. "She's right, Captain. Your time here is finished. You need to join your family."

As I spoke, the energy that had welled around him transformed to a glimmering wall. I'd seen that before with my Nana. It was The Veil separating the living from the next plane.

"You never answered my question. Who are you and where are ye from?" His voice was softer and I sensed his power waning.

"I'm Keira Swanson. I'm from Kingston." My head jerked back. Kingston? Where had that come from? I was from New York City!

"Aye. The first capital." He looked down at the floor. "I can't leave. This is my home. I built the bugger." He held up his hands. "With these hands, in a year, I laid each stone and cut every board! I'll not be leaving."

"You must leave, Captain. Your watch has ended. A family...a good family with children need this house. They'll take care of it." I reached for his hand. It was cold and....*spongy*. There, but not quite there. "I'll help you cross. I won't let go until you do. Your wife and children await."

His eyes narrowed at me. "So ye say." He shook his head. "I miss them something fierce." A sad smile spread on his lips.

"But aye, ye be right. Me watch is done. Time to cast off."

With his other hand, he gave a nod and half salute to Gwen before looking back at me. There was fear and sadness in his eyes. But something else. Resignation. He stepped over to the veil and peeked through.

Unlike the others I've seen cross, no joy covered his face. Instead, he shrugged, looked one last time to me, and stepped through, his hand slipping from mine.

My shoulders wracked and tears stung my eyes when he disappeared. I could feel the loss...his loss of his family, the loss of Mike Feeney. My loss of Nana. It all came out and I cried like a baby. Gwen's hand went over my shoulders and she hugged me, her tears mixing with mine. It was times like this when the immensity of life and death, the transition to the afterlife, hit like a sledge hammer, zapping every atom in my body...and Gwen felt it too.

We stayed like that for what seemed like hours but it was probably only five or ten minutes. Finally, she eased back and held me at arm's length. "It's done, Keira. I feel like I could sleep for days, but we did it."

I could only nod at her. We'd done it and I was totally drained.

"I'll check the rest of the house. We don't want to tell Stan it's over, if we haven't checked every room." She started to move to the living room and I trailed after her.

"But, we'd better do this together." I still wasn't sure she could sense spirits as well as I could.

She did an eye-roll but there was a smile on her face. "Oh ye of little faith."

"We'd better leave this village soon. You're starting to sound like Mrs. Kirkpatrick." I grinned and joined her in the living room.

She nudged me with her shoulder. "Honestly, what would you do without me?"

I clapped her on the shoulder. "Hopefully, we'll never know."

FIVE

Are you sure it's safe, now?" Maggie looked over my shoulder at the house, refusing to budge from her spot in the driveway. Her arms were crossed, with her hands tucked into the sleeves of her coat.

I grinned and let out a huge sigh, reaching for her arm. "We went through every room with a fine tooth comb. It's safe."

Gwen was standing on the stoop and she threw the door wide. "C'mon. We'll do a walk through with you, if you'd like."

My arm curled through Maggie's and I half dragged her up the walk to the stoop. She paused for a moment and her eyes were wide with fear. "You need to do more than that! Stay with us for a few days. There's plenty of room. I just don't—"

"Fine! We'll stay. When you're convinced it's okay, we'll go." I nudged her up the steps.

Behind me, Stan spoke up, his voice hesitant. "I don't know what to say. How much can I pay you for giving me back me home? Me life?"

I turned and let Gwen usher Maggie through the door. Stan and Maggie weren't well off and their thanks was all I wanted.

Lord knows, I had more money that I literally knew what to do with, thanks to Nana's will. Her legacy went above and beyond cultivating my paranormal abilities. Not only did she enlighten me to my destiny, she left me a gi-normous fortune. "Stan, just take care of the house. That's what Captain Smythe would want. That's all I ask."

"But what about the others? Those witches?" His jaw set tight, the muscle working. I didn't need to touch his hand to know how pissed he was that his daughter had been hurt and his family threatened.

"They were the first to leave. It was the Captain that wanted to linger." I smiled up at him. "But even he's gone now." I looked down the laneway where a group of people stood huddled in the chilly air. Two children, a young teenage girl in a ski jacket and jeans and a younger boy stood at the front of the crowd, staring at us. It was Emily and Robert waiting to get the all clear sign from their parents.

A half hour later, Stan and Maggie were on the front step waving the kids forward.

SIX

I t was two days after that, another crisp spring day, with a clear sky and Gwen and I were walking along the shoreline, skipping stones across the water and into the surf.

I tossed a big one in and turned to her, "I'm bored. I want to go home."

Her hands were thrust deep in her pockets, looking out over the water. Seagulls swooped low and then landed a few feet out. "I know, but Stan and Maggie might be offended. They're trying their best to make it up to us but I definitely agree with you. If I have to see Robert mooning over me, following me from room to room asking about my love life every minute, I'll go nuts."

I laughed. "He's got it bad for you, Gwen. There's a boy who likes older women!"

When she snorted, I decided to pry. Hey, what's life without a little of the dish? I nodded sagely and said, "I mean, Robert's just a kid, I don't think Roy would feel threatened." Call me immature if you want; I'm not above a good tease when it's called for. Besides, I was dying to know just how into Roy Gwen was. She played the cards of their relationship closer to her chest than a professional poker player.

One of the best perks of being an heiress is that I can fly anywhere I want at anytime I want. While Gwen and I were skipping stones into the ocean, a chartered plane was standing by at the St. John's International Airport four hours down the road. That plane had a pilot—the only one from the company I would use. And that pilot's name was Roy. He and Gwen hit it off big time. Just how big a time they were having was what I wanted to find out.

Considering my own love life was non-existent, I wasn't above scraping for some vicarious crumbs of romance, okay?

Gwen didn't say anything. She wouldn't look at me either. "Welllll?" I said.

When the blush crept up from her neck I knew I hit pay dirt. I nudged her with my elbow. "So... what *is* going on with you two?"

She chewed her lower lip and looked at me sideways. "He's funny and I can talk to him about interesting stuff. He's a friend, that's all."

My jaw dropped. "That's *it*? That's all you got for me?"

"Keira! Not everybody's like you!"

I scoffed. "No shit, Sherlock!"

"No! I don't mean..." she waved her arm back towards the house, "the ghost and goblin stuff, I mean..."

"You mean sex."

"No! I don't mean that! I mean..." she huffed a sigh. "I mean I move really, really slow when it comes to guys, okay?"

My eyes boggled. "You're saying I'm fast?" I blinked a couple of times. "You're saying I'm *easy*?"

"Oh for God's sake, Keira! I'm not saying *anything about you*! You were asking about *my* love life! I don't have a clue about your love life!"

"Okay, okay! Let's drop it then." Man, that wasn't fun at all. At. All.

"That's fine with me."

I bent over to pick up another stone. Keira eyed me and did the same. We stood there for a few minutes in silence just flinging stones out to the sea and let the squall between us settle down.

Flinging another stone, I said again, "I want to go home."

"Yeah, me too. I miss my Dad." Her father has MS and Gwen had been looking after him when we met last summer. After I found out about my legacy to become a 'Transitioner' or whatever, I hired Gwen to be my assistant. She's not a secretary; her main job is to watch my back when we go on these assignments. The proper term for her role is 'Guardian' believe it or not. My Nana had one—his name was Lawrence, and they both died the same day.

Gwen's biggest reservation about taking on this job was leaving her Dad alone. He's a widower and they're really, really close. Since we've been gone these last couple of weeks her aunt, his sister Elizabeth who's a retired nurse had been looking after him.

Elizabeth was not one of my favorite people. And Gwen disliked her even more.

Yeah, we were both itching to get back to Kingston.

I looked back at the house. "Stan and Maggie are trying to be great hosts, but they also want us to stick around 'just in case' y'know."

"In case those spirits come back, you mean?" Gwen asked.

"Yeah. They don't want us to go."

She nodded, and together we turned to head back to the house.

I made my way to the path leading to the old house. Maggie was a great cook and even though the room was cramped with the two single beds, it was clean and comfortable...but. I paused and looked around at Gwen. "I've got an idea. Maybe, we get them to *want* us to go."

Her face screwed into a knot of lines. "Good luck with that! They're tickled pink to *have* us here. How are you gonna pull that off?"

My grin was pure evil. "I'm thinking of giving Emily a make-over. Teach her about make-up and fashion." I turned and climbed up the path from the beach and Gwen's reply was almost lost in the wind off the water.

"She lives in a remote village. What does she need *that* for?"

When I reached the top, my plan was set. "Exactly." Her

face showed scepticism, standing next to me before we walked across to the house, and I smiled, "You've never seen me in Fifth Avenue, 'fashionista' mode, have you?"

***

Later that day, Stan jerked his head to the side, signalling for us to step outside to the stoop. Emily's whining filled the air as Maggie dragged her off to the bathroom. Emily was sporting nail polish, mascara, blush and lipstick, and Maggie was grumbling (and *not* quietly!) about scrubbing the war paint off.

I'd had the foresight to have our bags already packed and ready to go. We stepped outside and Stan's face was a mass of worry lines as he huddled close to us. "It's not that I don't appreciate what you've done here with the house and all....but, I think maybe—"

"We really should get back home, Stan." It was hard to keep the grin off my face when I looked at him. The relief in his softened features said it all.

He straightened and his head arched forward as he peered down the lane. "Now who's that comin' here, now?"

The round headlights of a black SUV threw gravel up behind it as it came up the drive. When it came to a stop beside our compact rental car, Roy got out. His blonde hair caught the glint of the setting sun and a broad smile was on his face as he strode forward.

"Keira! Hey Gwen!" His gaze rested on Gwen whose cheeks had turned a rosy shade of pink.

For a moment I was at a loss. What was he doing there? I turned to Stan, "This is our pilot, Roy."

"A pilot are ya?" Stan muttered, before extending his hand. "Hi, I'm Stan."

Roy shook it "Pleased to meet you." Immediately he turned to Gwen. "I got here as soon as I could. Are you two ready?"

I looked over at Gwen and my jaw dropped. She'd called Roy? Talk about 'oh ye of little faith'! She purposely didn't meet my eyes when she turned and raced back into the house.

I knew from the thud of her feet on the stairs inside, she was rushing to get our bags.

I smiled at Stan. "How about that, Stan? It seems we have to go anyway. Thanks for your hospitality the last couple of days. "I thrust my hand out and shook his. "Good luck. I'm sure you'll do well with this place." I looked out over the view of the ocean. "It's a magnificent spot."

Gwen burst through the door, laden down with our luggage and our coats.

Roy never missed a beat taking the bags from her and striding back to the SUV. I slipped my coat on and reached in the pocket for the car keys.

"Here's your hat, what's your hurry, eh?" Stan laughed and stepped down the stairs after me. He stood at the bottom and grinned. "Thanks again, Keira. Drive safe on the way back."

I waved to him and then stepped over to Roy who was loading the bags into the hatch door of the huge, beast of a vehicle. "Hey hotshot! What's with the rental? How'd you manage an Escalade? That's pretty rich, isn't it? "

He slammed the door shut and grinned at me. "Easy. I've got the company credit card."

My mouth fell open and I glared at him. "What? You mean MY credit card!"

His eyebrows bobbed high above blue eyes that laughed. "Exactly!" He glanced over at Gwen who was standing next to the passenger door. "You don't mind if Gwen rides with me, do you, Keira?"

The nerve of the guy! My credit card, carte blanche and now I had to ride alone on the four hour ride in a tin can compared to the luxury car! "Help yourself." I handed him the keys to the cramped compact, and snatched the Escalade's keys from his fingers. Edging by him, I opened the door and got in. My fingers fluttered in the window and the surprised look on Roy's face made me grin.

If I had to ride alone, there had to be some perks. I was footing the bill, after all.

SEVEN

I balanced the pizza box against my hip and slid the key into the lock. Home, after a three hour flight. Stepping inside the spacious foyer, I flipped the light switch and toed my shoes off. The place was really way too big for just me, but what the heck? Nana had wanted me to have it, along with her millions, so who was I to complain? Still...even my bare feet padding along the hallway to the kitchen echoed in the stillness.

After setting my pizza on the counter, I scooped my phone out of my bag and plugged it into the sound system. My favourite playlist began to blast and I couldn't help dancing and swaying as I pulled a slice of the pizza and threw it onto a plate. As I ate, I gazed around at the kitchen, at the stainless appliances, the granite counter and the small table next to the window. It was completely dark outside but there was no need to draw the curtain. My only neighbour out there was the expanse of lawn and the river.

At times like this I envied Gwen. I'd dropped her off at her Dad's house after we'd left the airport and got the pizzas.

Unlike here, there'd been lights shining in the downstairs, where her dad and aunt were probably watching TV. Even if her aunt irritated the hell out of her, at least she was there. And her dad? Forget about it. He'd be over the moon to welcome Gwen home.

I picked up my phone to check for email and any messages. There was one from Cerise as well as one from my mom. Cerise could wait. It was probably just an update on the bar scene and who was seeing who. I clicked the icon opening the one from Mom.

Hi Keira,
I hope you're taking care of yourself and remembering to eat a balanced meal every now and then.

I rolled my eyes munching on the pizza. It was balanced. There were mushroom and green peppers in the topping. What was she clairvoyant or just someone who knew me too well?

Call me when you get back from wherever the heck you are. I thought we could all get together for Easter. It might be nice if you came here and saw some of your old friends. Your Dad and I have decided to take a cruise this summer. Maybe Iceland or Alaska. You'd be welcome to join us if you can spare the time. LOL
Love
Mom

Getting away at Easter might be nice. But for now, I needed to recoup from the trip to Newfoundland. Nana had said that this house was a refuge that she'd used to kind of re-charge after doing a transition. I could totally get that. Even Gwen had been zoned out on the way home.

I finished the pizza and grabbed my phone along with a soft drink before plodding out of the kitchen and up to my room. Even though Nana and Lawrence had been gone for almost ten months, hanging around on the first floor—where we spent all our time together—still stung. I'll admit it; I still wasn't used to living here without them.

I had taken over the biggest room on the second floor and had it redecorated to my own tastes and style. It was now awash with cool blues and greens, from the bedspread to the curtains. It was a far cry from the bachelor hole in the wall apartment I'd had in Greenwich Village before I'd come here. This place was huge.

After I changed into my nightshirt and snuggled into bed, ready to answer some email, a new one had popped into my 'In' box. It was from Mr. Thompson. My shoulders slumped low and I sighed. I wasn't ready for another assignment yet. Whatever it was, would have to wait a few days. Just a few days to decompress...was that asking too much? And when I was rested, maybe a night out, dinner, dancing, having fun? Hell, I was only twenty-three. A girl needed to party a little too! Nana had in her younger days, so I should be able to as well.

I'd read his email tomorrow. I flipped to my streaming app and spent the next hour watching a couple of episodes of 'The Office', before drifting off to sleep.

***

The racket from a lawn mower right below my window woke me up the next morning. I pulled the pillow over my ears but the battle was lost when a vacuum in the hallway started. Oh maaan! It wasn't bad enough that the yard guys were here, but the cleaning lady showing up at the same time? It was no use. I tossed the covers back and checked the time. A quarter to nine. I should have left a message with the maid service, postponing their weekly visit. After all, I hadn't been home in almost three weeks! I needed a 'Lawrence', a guy Friday, to take care of these kinds of things. As well as looking after my Nana's safety, he was in charge of running the household. Maybe I could convince Gwen to move in since she was my Guardian? And take over this kind of stuff to boot? Yeah, fat chance. She was a 'Daddy's Girl' through and through.

I went into the attached bathroom and twenty minutes later I was downstairs eating left over pizza in the solarium at the back of the house. The scent of the flowers, mingled with the earthy soil smell always lifted my mood. No surprise; this had been a spot where Nana and I had spent many hours, as she tutored me in my psychic lessons. I sighed and took a seat at the small glass table, in the spot where she used to sit.

She was gone way too soon. There was still so much I needed to know and again, I sighed...I missed her. If only I'd met her earlier in my life instead of just in the past year. I opened the laptop, ready to answer Cerise's email and read the one from Mr. Thompson.

"Hey. How are you doing today?"

I jerked upright, staring at Gwen. Her cheeks were flushed and stray wisps of hair escaped the head band. She pushed the sleeves of her hoodie up her arms and took a seat across from me, still huffing from the run over.

"Mrs. Owens let me in." When she noticed my confusion, she added, "The cleaning woman. You know, the one you see every week." She shook her head, "Really, Keira?"

"What? I'm hardly even awake yet. Give me a break." I looked down at my breakfast."Would you like some pizza or a coffee?"

Her nose wrinkled and she sat back. "I had fruit and yogurt with Dad. I got out of there when Aunt Elizabeth decided to make him a..." her fingers formed quotation marks, "... 'healthy' breakfast of pancakes and sausage."

"Never one to be outdone, I see. Your poor dad. He rides a thin line between you two, keeping the peace." I took a sip of coffee and then looked at her over the brim, "What about you and Roy? How are things going on that front?" It was fun to watch her cheeks get pinker still.

She smiled and looked away for a moment, plucking a dead leaf from one of the plants next to her. "He's fun and interesting to talk to." She chuckled. "He told me a good joke." Her eyes fairly danced as she began, "A photon checks into a hotel. The bellhop asks, 'Can I help you with your luggage? It replies, 'I don't have any. I'm travelling light.'" A chuckle burst forth from her throat.

I could only stare at her. "Seriously? And you're laughing at that?" I took a bite of the pizza and shook my head. Trust a physics major to find that funny. Was Roy tickling more than her funny bone though? "So when are you seeing him again?" I tried to sound light, hiding the niggle of resentment that she had someone in her life, while I had nada.

She rose and began wandering around the room, inspecting and plucking dead leaves from the plants. "I don't know. He said he'd call the next time he was in town…that is, unless we get another transition case from Mr. Thompson."

I smacked my forehead. "Shit! He sent an email last night. I haven't even had a chance to read it yet."

Gwen twirled and her eyes were wide staring at me. It was hard to tell whether she was more excited about the assignment or seeing Roy again. "Let's read it. I hope it's not next week that we have to go." She pulled the chair up next to me so she could see the email as well.

"Why's that?"I clicked the mouse pad, watching the screen boot up. After a few more days alone in the house, I'd probably be ready for another trip out of town.

"It's Aunt Elizabeth. She mentioned this morning that she has to go back to Ottawa in a few days. Her daughter's going to give birth any day and she promised to help out with the baby." Gwen hunched forward in her chair, peering at the screen.

"You never mentioned she had kids. This would be your cousin?" I glanced over at her and then opened the email from Mr. Thompson.

"Yeah, I got a few."

My eyes were already scanning the email from Mr. Thompson.

We've received a request for help from a Nursing Home in Florida. It's a privately run five star

establishment, more like a country club than an institution. Apparently two of their clients passed away a few weeks ago and there's been a number of 'disturbances'. A number of their clients are threatening to leave if something can't be done about it quickly.

I realize this is short notice, especially after the affair in Newfoundland but you and Gwen are needed as soon as possible.

Please let me know if you have any interest in assuming this case. The address is 354 Russet Drive, Naples and the facility is 'Golden Acres'.

Sincerely,

Charles Thompson

I sat back and looked over at Gwen. "What do you think? It would be nice to get a jump on my tan this summer. Do some beach time...maybe even Disneyworld. That could be fun."

Her mouth fell open, staring at me. "Do you even *hear* yourself? This is a case, not a vacation! It must be pretty bad if some of their clients want to leave. Change isn't something elderly people like too much."

"Piece of cake! A couple spirits who probably didn't like the menu or the way they were treated and now are getting their revenge. Probably by the time we get there, they'll have left of their own accord." I laughed, "I don't care how posh the place is, it's still an institution with rules and schedules. Would you want to hang around there, if you were dead?"

She was quiet for a few moments, her teeth nibbling at her lower lip. "I don't know. I'd have to get Sean to come down from Toronto to look after Dad. It'd be short notice for him as well. He wasn't too thrilled with me taking this job with you and quitting the post office."

"He doesn't know what we do, does he?" Not even Gwen's dad knew what took Gwen and I out of the country for days at a time. He thought it was me looking after my late grandmother's business interests. Which was, if you think about it, kind of true. We just didn't get paid. Gwen's Dad was a great guy but this spook work would be a stretch for him to swallow. Not that I could blame him. I was still trying to get my head around the episode in Newfoundland. Ghosts *and* witch ghosts? "You haven't told your brother about all this stuff, have you?"

She rose to her feet and sighed. "No. If Sean knew, he'd have a stroke. I gotta get a glass of water. Be right back." Pausing in the doorway, she looked back at me. "Let me give Sean a call before you make any commitment to Mr. Thompson. Maybe he has some vacation time he hasn't used."

After she left the room, I sat back. It was hard to just take off at the drop of a hat with Gwen and her responsibilities. My grandmother had solved that problem with Lawrence living with her; her 'Guy Friday' assistant, as well as the love of her life who kept her bed warm. Nana had been lucky to have him. Why couldn't my 'Guardian' have been a single hottie, instead of Gwen? Life sucks, sometimes, but that's the way it goes.

I dashed off a quick reply to Mom about Easter, taking a pass on the invitation to the Alaskan Cruise. Eight months of cold weather was enough without squeezing it out on an Alaskan Cruise and with my parents to boot. The only cruising I wanted was the bar scene even if it was in this small city. I'd seen the military college on one of my trips to town. Surely they got out once and a while. Maybe Gwen would go with me.

She came back in the room, still holding the phone to her ear and slumping into the chair across from me. "It's only a week, Sean. When was the last time you spent any time with Dad?"

My eyes narrowed watching her wheedle and whine with her brother on the phone. It was ridiculous. Gwen had sacrificed her academic career, taking a job at the post office that allowed more time with her ailing father. Her brother had gotten off scot free in his family obligations. And what was a week anyway? The other time, we'd arranged for her Aunt

Elizabeth to be there, even if Gwen couldn't stand the woman. Sean was some selfish piece of work.

There was a silence and then she smiled. I could hear his voice even from where I sat, as he blared a 'fine!'

Her cheeks were flushed and her smile a bit tentative when she looked over at me. "He's coming. He had wanted to take a vacation in the summer and spend some time with Dad but, he's going to push that forward."

"Well, that's big of him" I clicked the mouse pad getting back to the email Mr. Thompson, to reply.

"Keira! It *is* a big deal! He has a job...you know, in the real world, nine to five with regular hours, a boss...all that kind of stuff. When was the last time you had a job, a real job?" She sat forward and her eyes were blazing over at me.

She didn't know it but she'd hit a soft spot. Before I'd come to visit my grandmother, I'd dropped out of three different programs in college and been fired from the only job I'd ever had—at a dry cleaners. But I wasn't going to go down that road with her. Instead, as usual my smart ass shone through.

"I don't need a regular job, do I? I'm worth millions and for your information the work we do is *more* important than delivering junk mail and bills. Or, in your brother's case making sure packages get through customs. Really! It wasn't like someone else can't take over Sean's work for a week."

"Yes. Thanks to your *grandmother*, you've got money and a career." Her voice was cold and she rose to her feet. "I'm going home. Let me know the details of when you want to leave for Florida. Take care." And with that she stalked through the doorway, leaving a cold silence behind her.

Shit! All I'd said was...I sighed. No. I'd said too much. She'd get over it though. I'd give her a day and then I'd go over to her Dad's house and apologize. Damned mouth! And all I'd wanted to do was relax and recoup my energy. Too bad my mouth hadn't stayed shut.

EIGHT

I spent the next two days basically sleeping and watching Netflix. Nana had told me that transitioning souls would be exhausting and she was right.

I hadn't heard a peep from Gwen. She didn't stop by, she didn't phone, nor did she so much as send a text.

But then, neither had I.

Just for the record, what she said to me really stung, okay? Up until the time I met Nana my life's accomplishments had added up to a big fat zero, and nobody knew that better than me. I'm 23, healthy as a horse and smarter than most people give me credit for. But with all my life's advantages, if I hadn't met Nana, I'd still be just another one of the club rats with a trust fund in New York; living my life at a hundred miles an hour and going nowhere fast. So Gwen's two cents worth about Nana rescuing my life really hit home.

But I had come back on her way, way too hard. Me and my big mouth.

On the third day I decided to straighten things out. I spent the morning on the phone getting the particulars of the trip to

MICHELLE DOREY

Florida organized. I'd use that as the excuse to go to her and smooth the troubled waters as soon as I got the chance. After a bite for lunch, I hopped into the Miata and five minutes later I was pulling into Gwen's driveway.

Gwen's aunt's car was still there along with a blue SUV. Before I could get out of the car, the door opened and a veritable Adonis stepped out on the veranda. I stopped breathing.

He had Gwen's chestnut hair, right down to the slight wave in it. But it was the blue eyes, deep set above sculpted, perfect cheekbones and a strong jaw that riveted me to the spot.

He continued down the steps, with the smooth athletic grace of a panther, tall, with broad shoulders that stretched the seams of his leather jacket. Instead of coming over to my car though, he went to the SUV and got a suitcase from the back. He barely glanced at me and then turned to sprint lightly up the stairs and into the house.

Hmph! Not even a wave or smile. I parked my car right behind his. Too bad if I was blocking him in! Gwen's aunt's car was free to leave as soon as she wanted to.

I tapped on the door and Gwen was there right away. She smiled a little ruefully as she opened the door wide. "Hey! C'mon in Keira."

"Hi Gwen. I hope this isn't a bad time but—"

"No, no. Sean's here and I want you to meet him." Her fingers tugged at the sleeve of my jacket.

Was she kidding? I wanted to meet him too! Thankfully, Gwen seemed like she got over our rift. Inside, the air carried a hint of cinnamon and I could see why when Elizabeth carried plates of apple pie to the living room.

She flashed a grin as she passed by Gwen and I, "You're right on time, Keira! I made a pie this morning in honour of Sean coming down from Toronto. I'll just have a piece with everyone and then I'm off. Did you hear I'm going to be a grandmother?"

Sean was nowhere to be seen. I plastered a smile on my face. "Yes! Congratulations, Mrs. Perkins! That's wonderful

40

news!" I made my way over to Devon and patted his shoulder, "How are you, Devon?"

"Better, now that you're here! It's great! Sean's home, Elizabeth is about to become a grandmother and now you're here. And the Jays beat the Yankees yesterday." His eyes gleamed up at me, trading barbs about our favourite baseball teams.

"Enjoy it while you can, Devon. The Jays winning streak can change in a New York minute." I took a seat and Elizabeth handed a plate with a piece of pie and fork on it. When I looked up at her, about to say thanks, a thought popped into my head. *She was going to angle her stepdaughter into making a granny suite in her home.*

I mumbled a 'thanks' but my mind was racing ahead at ninety miles an hour. I hadn't touched Elizabeth's hand and yet I'd been able to read her thoughts! Up to that point I'd had to touch a person to get any kind of insight. My powers were growing! I couldn't wait to get Gwen alone and tell her.

I looked over at Devon to try to discern his thoughts. He *was actually happy about getting a break from his sister Elizabeth. Her constant chatter, the back biting and slags on Gwen were starting to get to him*! Gwen looked over at me and again thoughts jumped unsolicited into my head. *She was still annoyed with me, and it was the prospect of seeing Roy again, rather than the assignment in Florida that was making her soften towards me.*

"Keira? Are you okay?" She took a seat next to me on the sofa.

Before I had a chance to answer, Sean came into the room, all six foot four of oozing male hotness. He had a button down shirt, but the top two buttons were undone. That look on a guy always turned my head, but in this case my knees quivered. Not a lot, but yeah, they did. I was glad I was sitting down. When he looked over at me with those exquisite blue eyes of his, I focused on his thoughts.

Pink elephants. The image flashed in my brain and refused to leave. What the hell? I was just trying to get a reading from him but instead pink elephants were lumbering in my head.

"Sean, this is Keira Swanson. Keira, my brother, Sean."
Gwen's voice barely penetrated past the elephants.

I smiled and waited for him to step forward to shake my
hand. I could hardly wait to touch his skin. Did he think I was
as hot as I thought he was? His hotness must have fried my
brain so I could only think of pink elephants. With him, I
needed to actually touch him. And oh man, did I want to touch
him...

Instead of stepping over and shaking my hand, he put his
hands on his waist and said, "So, you're Gwen's new friend
and employer? I have you to thank for screwing up my
vacation plans?" His voice was even and his look steady and
cool. He looked over at his father and his smile warmed the
frosty air around him, "Not that it's not great to see you Dad,
it's just that I'd wanted to come this summer and get some
things done around here. Fix the floor in the shed and patch
the roof. Things that Gwen can't manage on her own." He
made a moue with his mouth and looked out the window. "It's
too wet and cold to do that work this time of year."

My cheeks got hot. Not only did he not bother shaking my
hand but he was giving me shit for the Florida assignment?
Who the hell did he think he was, anyway? He was probably
used to women falling all over themselves trying to get next to
him. Fine!

I turned to Gwen, "Roy is picking us up at the airport
tomorrow at eleven. We'll be in Florida by three." That should
make her happy that I'd managed to get Roy as one of the
pilots in the chartered plane.

Her face screwed up. "Tomorrow? I was hoping to have a
day with Sean."

In the background, Elizabeth tsked and muttered, "Now
Gwen, don't look a gift horse..."

Before she could even complete that, Sean broke in,
"That's right, Gwen! The boss lady says jump and you say how
high?" He cut a piece of the wedge of pie on his plate with his
fork, scowling over at his sister.

Devon squirmed forward. "Sean, There's no need to—"

"Well, Keira might be Gwen's boss but she's not mine. I think it's ridiculous that Gwen took this job. Her degree is in physics not being a personal assistant to some rich kid." He stared at me, daring me to answer. The cards, as far as he was concerned were on the table.

The silence in the room was as taut as the skin of a balloon with that last straining puff of air. I smiled sweetly, using every thread of control in my body, "Gwen is more than a 'personal assistant'. I rely on her advice and judgement. You underestimate her, Sean. Even as a physicist, she couldn't prove any more beneficial, in the work we do together." There. It was vague but there was no way he was tricking me into letting the cat out of the bag.

"Sean, it's fine. I *want* to work with Keira." Gwen tried to break the tension that was getting higher, when Sean glared at me.

"Gwen, you may have been bought off by Keira's money, but I think it's a mistake. You were happy when it was just you and Dad. Now, everything's in a state of flux, dependant on Keira's whims. I had plans for doing things around here this summer. It's not like I can just up and leave my job on a dime." His words and eyes were chips of ice.

"Why not work in Kingston to be closer to your father? There're jobs here. Hell! If it's that important to get these things done around here, I can pay you." I reached for my purse, "I'll write you a check right now." If he was making this such a big deal, I'd call his bluff. Plus, if it would get him here to help with Gwen's dad, it would simplify things, even if he was a total jerk to be around.

"I'm not for sale. You may impress Gwen and Dad but I can see right through you. If you ask me, you have a lot of growing up to do, little girl."

Whoa! *Little girl?* What the hell was with him? He had a serious chip on his shoulders and he was knocking it off at me. I swallowed my reply for the sake of Gwen and Devon. If this was anywhere else, it would have been war.

Elizabeth rose to her feet, "I really should get going. The

traffic will be awful if I wait any longer." She reached for Devon's pie plate and took it into the kitchen.

"Sean. You're being rude. Keira is a nice girl." Devon had turned fifty shades of red looking down at his lap.

I stood up. "It's okay, Devon. Actually, I might have blocked Elizabeth in and should move my car." I lied, turning to Gwen, "I'll see you tomorrow." On my way out, I squeezed Devon's shoulder. As I passed Sean, my face twisted into a smile that I didn't feel in my gut, "Nice to meet you, Sean."

There was no way I was going to add to Gwen's or Devon's discomfort but boy oh boy, would it be nice to get that asshat alone and give him a piece of my mind. He didn't know who he was dealing with when he met me. If I'd wanted to, I could have caused his pie to grind into his face with the twitch of an eyebrow. Well, maybe.

Gwen got up and walked with me to the door. "See you tomorrow. I'll catch a ride to the airport with Sean."

My heart sunk as I slipped my shoes on. Some sort of apology might have been nice. Instead, she'd made it a point to let me know that blood was thicker than water.

As I drove back to the empty house, I'd never felt so alone.

NINE

I waited in the lounge area of the airport, feeling like a Mac Truck had driven over me and then backed up to finish me off. Too many gimlets while Skyping with Cerise after I got home from Gwen's. I owed Cerise a call and what better way to vent how pissed off I was after the encounter with Sean? She'd agreed. He was a total jerk, not worthy of any more attention. I didn't get into how disappointed in Gwen I was. Cerise wouldn't get that and there was no way I wanted to explain.

The door from the tarmac opened and Roy walked into the lounge, gazing out the glass wall for any sight of Gwen. He really had it bad for her.

They'd make an odd couple. She had to tower over him by a good four inches and while she was a lithe brunette, he was stocky with a hank of unruly blonde hair. He was always cracking jokes, while Gwen was more serious and reserved.

"So, do I get the credit card on this trip? I could have a blast at Epcot. I love Disneyworld." He glanced at his watch. "Where is she? We're due to take off in ten minutes."

"Shhh...not so loud. My head is killing me. She'll be here. Her brother is driving her." I looked up at him, hating the fact that his eyes were a clear blue and his skin was freshly scrubbed, the all American guy, while I felt like last week's soup, green and sickly.

His voice was chipper, drilling into my ear canals when he spoke, "There she is!" He looked like a puppy dog watching her and her brother come down the corridor. I sighed. It'd be nice to have a guy look at me like that. I focused on him just for a second. *He wanted to go on the 'It's A Small World' ride with her at Disneyworld? And hold her hand?* That was too much. Talk about sweet and innocent! How old was Roy? Eight?

I took a quick peek into Gwen. *She REALLY hoped Sean would like Roy.*

She cast an almost shy smile at Roy. "Hi Roy. She pulled her brother by the arm. "Sean, this is Roy Kinsley. Roy, my brother Sean."

Sean reached out and shook Roy's hand. "Hey man, good to meet you. Gwen thinks you're pretty cool." Still pumping hands, he glanced out the window to the tarmac where our Citation was parked. "You're flying that? Whoaa..."

Roy stood up a little straighter. "Well, not by myself; it has a crew of two and my co-pilot's in the cabin pre-flighting."

Sean released his hand. "Flying for a living, huh? Man that's cool."

Roy went into self-effacing mode. "It's a good job. What I really like doing is taking out a single engine prop and playing Yank and Bank. Now *that's* fun!"

Sean leaned in. "What's 'Yank and Bank'?"

"We're a group of former Naval Aviators. We play mock dogfights. Think of Laser Tag in the sky."

Gwen piped up. "Roy was a fighter pilot for the Navy, Sean."

Sean's eyes boggled. "No way!"

Roy gave a little shrug. "Yeah. I was. I lost flight status when I had to eject after a bad launch." He bent and slapped his knee. "Bashed my knee up just bad enough to disqualify for combat ops." He straightened up and gazed at Gwen. "It was all for the best, I think." They stared at each other in swimming silence for a moment, blocking out the rest of the world.

Sean cleared his throat, and Roy looked over to him. "Y'know, the Yank And Bankers got one of our things coming up. The plane I use has two seats up front..."

"You're inviting me?" Sean said. Geez! Now it was Sean's turn to look like a kid!

"Yeah! They're a lot of fun. It'd be cool."

"Sure, bro!" Sean stuck his hand out again. "That's awesome!"

I didn't have to read Gwen's mind; the look on her face told everything. Roy had gotten the 'Sean Stamp of Approval' and she was elated.

But *me*? I was paying his sister a million bucks a year, *and* covering the expenses for her home and he treated me like some kind of bug and she couldn't care less!

I bit my tongue and got to my feet. I handed my bag to Roy, just in case he forgot who he was working for. "Hey Gwen. We'd almost given up on you. Roy is chomping at the bit to get going."

Sean flashed a scowl my way. I stared right back at him, trying to discern what was going around in that head of his. I reached for Gwen's suitcase which Sean held in his hand, purposely brushing my fingers along his. *The butcher shop for steak, propane for the BBQ,...skanky bitch is hung over, probably spent the night with some loser,...and yeah, sour cream for the potatoes.*

My eyes widened looking at him. What the hell? A shopping list interspersed with a slag on me? The bastard! Who was he to judge me? I huffed a sigh through pinched nostrils, ready to put this jerk in his place. "Hey you—"

"I'll get that." Roy edged forward cutting off my words and line of sight on the big asshat, taking the suitcase from my hand. "We'd better get going, Keira. I have a filed flight plan and the FAA's pretty particular about schedules."

Gwen gave Sean a kiss on the cheek while I shot daggers

with my eyes meeting his. When he smirked at me, I responded. It was a reflex. I lifted my hand, my middle finger spiking up from my closed fist before I spun to follow Roy.

"Is she always this juvenile, Gwen?" He said it out loud.

I marched out the door to the tarmac, cutting off any other rude thing he wanted to say. What the hell was his problem anyway?

Gwen's feet pattered quickly behind me. "What was that all about? Flipping him the bird like that?"

I climbed the steps, feeling my blood boil despite the nip in the air. I could hear Gwen's thoughts and they weren't pretty. She was *totally* taking his side, thinking I was being a snarky bitch. I tried to remind myself that she didn't know the nasty comment his mind had hurled at me. I entered the cabin and then threw my handbag on the seat.

"Your brother hates me for no reason. From the moment he laid eyes on me, he's been rude! Don't forget that I read minds Gwen. I know what he thinks of me. And actually, I know what you're thinking too! I don't have to touch people to pick up their thoughts anymore." I plopped into the plush leather seat and reached for the seat belt.

"What are you talking about? You have to do a whole 'focus' exercise and touch them!"

I shook my head. "Not anymore."

"Wait a second. You can read my thoughts right here? Right now?" When I nodded, she continued. "You can enter my head whenever you want? Know every secret thing I'm thinking?" She blanched as she took as seat across from me and snapped the seat belt shut. Her eyes were flinty. "That's just wrong, Keira! You have no right to do that whenever you please."

"I have every right! You work for me, remember?" It was out before I could even think about it. From the shocked look on her face, I knew I'd gone too far. "Look, I'm not trying to invade your privacy or—"

"Sure looks like it to me! But then, you're already acting like you own me, so that makes it all right, in your books." Her fingers thrummed on the table and she turned to stare out the window at the tarmac that was rumbling by, faster and faster.

Numbers invaded my head. Equations and formulas. Pi, infinity, square roots. She was blocking me! Thinking of mathematics and physics, as a way to hide her true thoughts. But the feelings, *the rage* was still coming through.

Fine! I yanked my bag from the seat beside me and got my Kindle eReader. If she was going to play that game, I could too! After we lifted off I spent the next half hour reading, occasionally glancing over at her. The numbers were waning and she was second guessing whether she should have left the job in the Post Office.

When Roy opened the door to our cabin, we both turned to look at him. "How is everything back here? We're going to be hitting some turbulence in another ten minutes. I was going to suggest buckling up, but I see you've got that covered."

"Oh you didn't need to tell us that. Keira knew. She knows *everything*, Roy." Gwen's smile was ice cold.

"Thanks, Roy," I said

Roy's gaze pinged between Gwen and I for a few volleys. I picked up *'Uh oh, cat fight'* before he cleared his throat. "I'd better go up front again." He made a quick and quiet escape.

"Can I ask you to do me a favour?" Gwen's eyes narrowed when she looked over at me.

"I won't purposely read your thoughts. I may have to plug my ears and hum a tune, but I'll try. That's all I can do. That was what you wanted to ask me." I slumped lower in the chair and gazed out the window. "Your brother is really being a jerk to me though, Gwen. Even your dad called him on it yesterday."

"Do I have to speak or are you just going to invade my mind whenever you want?" Gwen clicked the seat belt open and then rose to her feet. "I'm going to the rest room." She did a face palm. "Silly me. You already knew that!"

That and the fact that she was contemplating taking the next flight back to Kingston when we landed.

***

We were on our way to the hotel in our rental and I knew I had to clear the air, at least until we finished this case at the Nursing Home. The way it was looking, it would be our last case together, if I didn't make some sort of attempt. And really, we had gotten along fine until her asshat brother showed up.

"Gwen, we need to talk. And I'll ignore the come-back that just flashed in your head. I'm not trying to invade your privacy. Believe it or not, it makes me uncomfortable too. I mean, because it's you." I looked over at her and managed a small smile. "Any ideas how we're going to get around this? I'm open to your thoughts." I groaned. "Poor choice of words."

"I'll say!" But she smiled. "This is huge for me, Keira. I've always been a very private person and now, even my thoughts are on display. It's like you're reading my diary! Actually it's worse! I can't keep reciting math formulas in my head to block you."

"It works though. You'd put me to sleep with that crap."

"So does this work with everyone you meet?" She pointed at the other cars on the road. "What about that cab driver over there? Or all the people at the airport? I would think that sensing all those thoughts would drive you crazy."

Now that I was aware of the cab driver, I mean *consciously* aware, my head was filled with how he hoped the Marlins were going to beat the Yankees next week.

I turned to her again, "When I focused on him, his dominant thoughts came through clear as a bell. But you're right about the airport. I didn't get a huge deluge of random thoughts. So, this ability is still something I have to consciously use."

"So you do have control of this. Maybe, where I'm concerned you could just not invade my head and my privacy?"

I smiled. "Maybe..."

"KEIRA!" She turned and stared straight ahead.

"I was kidding! Look, I'll try but this is new to me too. We have an appointment to see the owners of the nursing home tonight."

"We're going out there, *tonight*?" Her face fell.

She'd made plans with Roy for the evening. I didn't need to read her mind to know that. Her face was an open book right then. "Yes, at seven. I think we need to be there at night and assess what's going on, don't you? The sooner we meet with them and take care of this the better."

"Yeah, I guess." She reached in her purse and pulled out a folded sheet of paper and passed it to me. "I did some research on the place. Three weeks ago, two residents died the same day. Abigail Stettler and Brian Pugsly. There's been no other deaths since and the most recent before these two croaked, was four months ago. So I think these two must be the culprits creating havoc."

"That's weird that they died the same day...do you think something was wrong with their tapioca puddings?" Or maybe their meds got mixed up?" The print of the obituary clipping showed a plump, elderly woman laughing in a candid shot while the thin face of the old man looked like he'd eaten a crate of lemons.

Gwen sighed. "I'm sure that sort of thing happens more than you'd guess. How about we meet in the lobby at 6:30? I'm meeting Roy in a half hour." Her eyebrow arched, "Not that I had to tell you that."

"I wasn't doing anything, Gwen!"

"How would I know?"

This was going to be a 'thing' that we'd either have to figure out how to deal with or call it quits. The way I was feeling right then—still hung over and feeling sorry for myself—it wouldn't matter one way or the other. This was going to be our last assignment together; I could feel it.

TEN

W hoaaa... this place is *nice.*"
    We had just arrived at our latest assignment, the
nursing home with two freeloading residents. Okay,
maybe they were ghosts, but they weren't paying any fees,
right?

After being buzzed through the front gates, we proceeded
up a long, meandering driveway lined with stately oak trees.
The residence was set back in a park-like setting with a pond,
an expanse of trimmed lawn bordered by cypress and palm
trees. The sun was a crimson orb sitting low on the horizon as
we left the car and walked to the entrance. It was a grand old
southern home reminiscent of Tara, in *Gone with the Wind,*
replete with the pristine white Grecian columns, and an
oversized sleepy veranda on each side leading down to
manicured flowery gardens. There was nothing sterile and
institutional about this place. You could tell it cost a pretty
penny to live here. Golden Acres was aptly named.

Gwen pressed the doorbell and then glanced over at me.
"This place is pretty exclusive. You'd never know it, but there

are fifty suites in the main building and twenty private bungalows. There's a waiting list to get in here."

"But, if there's a wait to get in here, why are they so concerned about this haunting?" I peered around at the property, noting the park benches and pergola off to the side.

"That's just it...word gets around and they want to stifle any rumours before they start hurting them financially."

That made sense. Nip any stories in the bud before they got out of hand.

The door opened and a middle aged man in a casual and *expensive*, Ralph Lauren sweater, and dark pants ensemble did a double take, staring at us. "Ms. Swanson, Ms. Jones?" He smiled and held the door wide for us to enter. "Sorry, I guess I was expecting older people."

"I get that a lot, I hope I grow out of it," I said as I swept by him.

When I entered, I took stock of him and the woman who rushed over to join us. She was his wife and equally concerned to see that we looked so young. I hadn't exactly dressed the part of psychic investigator in my cotton capri's and a slouchy blouse, but Gwen was in tailored pants and shirt. Naturally, he assumed that Gwen was the senior partner, extending his hand to her.

I shook the woman's hand and introduced myself. "I'm Keira Swanson. You contacted me through my attorney, Mr. Thompson."

The woman's eyes flashed wide for a moment as she looked at Gwen and then back to me. She smiled, "I'm Carol Barnes. I'm so glad you were able to make time for us on such short notice."

As we shook hands, I said, "And this is my associate, Gwen Jones."

I turned to the guy, and shook his hand. He introduced himself as Jarrod Barnes. "We just got back from an assignment off the east coast of Canada. I'm sure that Mr. Thompson discussed our fee with you?"

"Yes, yes. My wife and I have owned this home for years. I

must say, this is the first anything like this has ever happened." His hand lingered in mine for a beat too long. We might look inexperienced in dealing with the spirit realm, but we were just about the right age for this letch.

Gwen stepped forward, gazing around the foyer that split off into a myriad of rooms, before she turned to Carol. "Tell us what has been happening and then we'll need to see the rooms."

She'd picked up on the sleaziness of the guy as well.

Carol cleared her throat and led the way to an office tucked into one side of the entrance. "It's been happening in the main building where the residents require more medical supervision."

"What, like a hospital?" Gwen asked. She was taking the lead in the questioning, which was fine by me.

"Nursing home. We have three sections; 'Retirement Living', 'Assisted Living' and 'Nursing Home'. As our clients decline, they are able to go from one mode of living to the next."

With the last stage being out the door to a Funeral Home. I glanced over at Gwen. We both were thinking of her dad.

"So what happened?" she asked.

"As we outlined to Mr. Thompson, two long term clients died within minutes of each other. Since that night, the overnight nursing staff and security have seen strange things happen."

"Like what?"

Carol looked away. "This may not sound strange to you, after all it's what you deal with all the time I suppose. But it *is* odd nevertheless. We've had doors open on their own, the fire alarm's gone off without anyone touching anything, and items from residents' rooms have gone missing to appear in the oddest of places."

Gwen nodded. "That sounds strange enough to me."

"Not to mention the complaints of sudden chills that a few of the other residents experience." Jarrod added his two cents to the conversation. He wrinkled his nose. "And the God awful smells that come up for no reason!"

"How did they die? Was there any connection between the two deceased?"

I'd picked up on the flash of fear in Jarrod's mind when she'd asked the question. Then an image of a red headed nurse, her lipstick smeared and her top gaping open to reveal a lacy bra flashed from his comb-over head. That was how the two residents had died. The nurse and Jarrod were involved in some kind of sneaky affair and she'd missed giving the two patients their meds while they were making whoopee in a store room.

Jarrod's face had flushed. I spoke up. "We'd like to see the rooms. Has the visitations been more frequent with some staff over others?"

Again the slippery guilt threaded through Jarrod's mind but it was Carol who answered my question.

"Jeanine Worthington seems to be particularly affected. I've noticed that when she's scheduled for the graveyard shift, there're more complaints." She gazed at me, "You think that she's some kind of magnet for this?"

I picked up on the images in both of the owners' minds. Carol had her own suspicions about Jeanine, the red headed nurse. She'd caught her husband checking the woman out on more than one occasion and given his history... For his part, Jarrod couldn't wait for this to end.

"Why don't we visit the rooms? Keira will be able to assess this more closely once she's there. I take it all of the personal belongings of Abigail and Brian have been removed?"

"Well, Abigail's family cleared her room out the day after she died, but Brian had no family. We left his room alone as soon as this craziness started." Carol walked to the door, leading the way to the elevator across the spacious foyer.

Jarrod cleared his throat and moved behind the desk, taking a seat. "I'll just stay here. There's a bit of work I need to finish off. Carol can take care of anything you need."

I paused before leaving to join Gwen and Carol, fixing a small smile on my face as I stared at him. The man was as guilty as the nurse in causing the premature deaths of the two residents and now was too chickenshit to go anywhere near the rooms.

He was scared to death of ghosts, yes; but more than that was worried if they would tell us what had really happened. Poor guy didn't realize I already knew the whole story. I left him there and walked over to the elevator and joined the others.

The first room was fairly spacious, with a hospital bed and a sitting area for visitors. Even though it had been stripped of personal effects in preparation for the next resident, I sensed Abigail lingering. As I walked over to the bed, her form began to shimmer like threads of silver, sitting on it.

Behind me, Gwen was murmuring to Carol, dismissing her for us to do the work in this room and the one next to it— Brian's. After a few moments, Gwen was beside me, her hands running briskly up her arms.

"It's cold in here." She looked around, oblivious to the spirit that was now gazing at me. She took a deep breath. "It's hard to breathe too."

I barely heard her, my eyes fixed on the apparition on the bed. "Abigail Stettler?" I watched the entity nod slowly. The poor woman had been looking forward to her eighty-fifth birthday. Her family had planned a party with her grandchildren and nieces and nephews. But she'd been denied that occasion when Jeanine had missed her heart meds.

Her woe emanated from her almost like a fragrance. She wasn't ready to move on when she died! Why should she be denied that one last kiss, that one last hug from her children and loved ones? It wasn't fair! My own chest ached. I could feel the pain wracking her body, her fingers scrambling for the call button before falling away.

"You can see her?" Gwen asked.

I nodded in reply, not taking my eyes from Abigail's. "I'm sorry you missed your party. But it's time to leave this place." My hand drifted to the shimmering waves that were Abigail and tears filled my eyes as I experienced her sadness. There was no anger, which was what I would have expected, just deep sorrow. Her only daughter dominated her emotions.

"Your husband is waiting, Abigail. John..." His name came to me in a flash. "John is just over there." She turned and it was then that the shimmering Veil of light appeared. "Your daughter loves you but she takes comfort in the thought that you've joined her father again. It's time."

She nodded and her form rose from the sofa, drifting closer to the wave of pure energy. She smiled at me and then stepped forward and through the curtain. The Veil faded quickly after she left.

This one, Abigail hadn't been the spirit creating havoc in the home. She'd needed just a nudge to get her to go where she belonged. Something told me, Brian Pugsly wouldn't leave so easily.

ELEVEN

I turned to Gwen. "She's gone. You know what happened here don't you?" The air in the room was already warming and it was easier to breathe. I looked around and then stepped next to my partner.

"I didn't see her...not like the last time when we at the Smythe house." Gwen's forehead was tight as she stared at me.

"Abigail was a frail, sweet spirit. She was faint, so it's no wonder you didn't get a sense of her, aside from the way the room felt." We walked out of the room and closed the door behind us. The corridor was empty; no one else was around.

We walked along the corridor until we came to the door to Brian's room. "Carol left it unlocked for us." Gwen turned the handle but the door refused to budge. "There's something pushing against it on the other side," she said in a whisper.

I stood beside her and watched as she put her shoulder to it. Slowly it opened a crack and a waft of foul, freezing air slithered out into the hall. My hand slid into my pocket and closed around the black tourmaline stone. "Brian Pugsley, we're here to help you," I said , keeping my voice low.

"Brian's not here. He died."

I jumped at the sound of the voice breaking the still air. When I turned, the door across the hall from where we stood was open and an elderly black woman in a silk dressing gown leaned out the door. Her eyes were narrow slits, "But you knew that, didn't you? Who are you and what would you want with Brian?" Her fingers tightened on the side of the door.

"Carol and Jarrod asked us here. Have you seen any odd things happen around here?"

The old lady had seen plenty. She'd been wondering about the noises coming from his room and the foul stench. She also knew that the owner and that red headed bitch had been responsible for Brian's death. Not that she missed the old fart. He'd always been cranky and hard to get along with.

All this flared in my mind before the old woman had a chance to answer. Before she could say a word, we were interrupted by the elevator opening and a certain red haired nurse stepped out. Quick as a flash, the old woman's door snapped shut.

A scornful look crossed the features of her heavily made up face. There was a lot of hard living under that foundation, rouge and lipstick. Replace her scrubs with jeans and a leather jacket, and she would fit right in at a biker bar. She spoke with a raspy voice. "So you're the ghost whisperers? How much is Carol paying you for your tricks?" Her arms crossed over an ample bosom and she shifted her weight to one hip, a smirk on her lips.

The door that Gwen had managed to pry open a few inches slammed shut, the noise bouncing off the walls and through my feet. Brian wasn't too happy to see this nurse.

I took a step closer to her until we were almost nose to nose. "Jeanine Worthington. The same woman who stopped taking birth control a few months ago. Jarrod is your last shot at hitting the good life, right? Too bad about the two abortions you had. Your chances of trapping a guy with pregnancy are pretty well shot." My eyes narrowed. "Not to mention at 41 years old, the odds weren't in your favor to start with."

Her eyes boggled and I stormed on. "Yeah, I know; everyone thinks you're 32." I did my best chicken head. "But we know that's a lie, don't we? I suggest you make yourself scarce while Gwen and I employ our 'tricks' here." I tilted my head to the room door. "Brian Pugsley knows what really happened and so do I."

Her face blanched and the sneer became an 'Oh shit!' look. The change in her expression made my heart swell. I spun around and gripped the handle of the door, easily opening it and stepping inside. Gwen was right on my heels.

I looked around and sniffed at the rank smell of decay. All his belongings were still here—a bathrobe was draped over one of the chairs and a bookcase was against the wall. "You liked that, Brian? I know about 'Nurse Ratched' and Jarrod. I don't blame you for being pissed."

Books flew from the bookcase and slammed to the floor. Brian was showing off, letting us know that he was no weakling like Abigail.

It was time to let him know he'd met his match. I focused on the books littering the floor and one by one, they rose in the air and slid back onto the shelves. Well, all but one, which overshot the mark and landed on top of it. Still, my telekinesis was improving. I hadn't broken the window!

"Good work, Keira." Gwen glanced over and then her fingers closed over the rosary, holding it high.

Promptly, one of the books from the shelf was hurled at me. When I ducked out of the way it stopped in mid-air. I straightened up and it dodged at me again, stopping an inch from my nose, making me squeak. Yes, I squeaked. Sue me. It floated in the air, and then drifted gently to the floor. I bent and picked it up. It was an old copy of *The Turn of The Screw* by Henry James.

I shrugged. Never heard of it. I tucked it under my arm and looked around the room. "Okay, you won that one. Thanks for not bopping me, I guess." I took a long measured breath. Before I had a chance to do anything else, the bed began bouncing, the metal legs jarring the floor, beating a fast rhythm.

I felt Gwen's hand on my arm and we stepped forward, both of us avoiding the bed. "Brian Pugsley, that's enough!" The bed fell onto the floor with a loud clunk.

A piercing bell blared from the hallway, followed by a woman's shrill shrieks. I knew that it was the bitch nurse who was stuck in the elevator.

"Brian! You have to stop this!" My heart galloped like a racehorse in my chest as I gazed around at the room. "Show yourself!" The hair on the back on my neck spiked high and I could feel him laughing at me. It was obvious why he'd never had many friends in the nursing home. He was one cantankerous S.O.B..

The air over the bed wavered like a road mirage on a hot summer day. A shape formed slowly on it. When it came fully visible, my eyes almost popped out of my head. The old man patted the spot beside him and smiled.

He was completely naked.

"You've *got* to be kidding!" The first proposition I'd had in months is from a naked old ghost? I shook my head and muttered, "I really have to work on my social life."

At Gwen's giggle, I spun to face her. "It's not funny!"

"C'mere, cutie pie," Brian said. There was a sly humour in the ancient voice.

No way was I playing his game! I pulled the stone from my pocket and strode over to stand in front of him. I wasn't backing down. "Brian, you need to go. You've had your fun, but there's no place for you here anymore."

The entity rose to its feet, invading my space, sending rank chills through my body. But I stood my ground, my jaw clenching so hard it ached. He wasn't malevolent, just an ornery old coot. Next to us, The Veil began to shimmer and take shape. "Go through The Veil, Brian. You had a hard life here but your friend...Bert... is over there. Join him and know the peace you never had on this plane."

His hand rose and it was like ice drifting over my cheek. But I sensed a weakening in his resolve to stay here.

"You remember the times you had together...the practical jokes and the laughs. He was your only true friend and he's over there."

My words were having an effect on him. He turned his gaze over to the shimmering silver web of light and his hand left my face. Now just a final push...."Your parents and sister also are there for you, Brian."

He turned his head to The Veil and then back at me. His face sparked into a jesting expression and before I could react he jerked forward and planted a frosty kiss on my cheek! Eeew! In a single move he pivoted and stepped through The Veil.

My eyes closed and I exhaled a huge breath only then aware I'd been holding it. It was over. Definitely not one of the nicer transitions. Kissed by a naked ghost. Ewwww!

Gwen stepped closer and her hand gripped mine. "That was weird. Even for us." She walked back to the door and cocked her ear, trying to hear what was happening outside in the hall. She looked over at me and smiled. "All quiet, now."

My hands clutched the tourmaline stone tight and then I slipped it in my pocket again. "We're done here."

When we got downstairs again, the only person waiting was Carol. Jarrod and nurse Ratched were nowhere to be seen, which was fine by me. I walked over to her and spoke softly. "They're gone now, Carol."

She grasped my hands in hers. "Really? You're sure?"

"Yes."

"Oh thank you! Thank you!"

"But...your problem isn't. Get the best lawyer you can find and buy Jarrod out. You can do better than a sleaze-ball like him."

Her face took on an embarrassed look. "Because of that floozy?"

"Yes."

She looked away for a moment and back to me. "No."

"What? He cheated on you!"

"I know, dear. He's also been a loyal and true husband for more than twenty years." When I started to reply, she put a finger on my lips. "Now shush. You don't throw the baby out with the bathwater, Keira. Jarrod was stupid, yes; but everyone does stupid things now and then, don't they?"

I closed my mouth and nodded.

"It's going to be a delicate thing to get that floozy out of here. Jarrod has left us wide open for a sexual harassment lawsuit."

"Now *that* I can help with. Nurse Worthington's real name is Laura Downes. She's not an RN. She stole the identity of the real Jeannine Worthington three years ago. Not only can you fire her, you can have her arrested if you want."

Carol's eyes flew open wide. "Really? How do you know?"

"Let's just say she let the cat out of the bag when we met up at Brian's room."

"I'll make her leave quietly then." Carol looked around the building. "Jarrod and I have our whole lives invested here. I don't know how to thank you."

I chuckled. "Make him pay a price for cheating and I'll be happy."

Her eyes narrowed in an evil grin. "I said I would forgive him. But that doesn't mean he's not going to pay for being stupid!"

We both laughed, and that was that.

TWELVE

We spent the next couple of days in Florida. I say 'we' but it was actually more like me going to the beach, shopping and sightseeing on my own, while Gwen and Roy did their thing together. Whenever I chanced upon them in the lobby or outside on the street, Gwen clammed up tighter than an oyster, running through recipes, math equations and even singing songs lyrics in her head.

So much for a vacation. It was a tense few days. Things were coming to a head between Gwen and I over my ability to read minds. I figured that we'd work it out when we got back home. Just how, I didn't have a clue; but I had faith that we'd fix this issue between us.

I couldn't have been more wrong.

It all fell apart when we were checking out of the hotel. She was standing beside me while I settled up the bill.

'Stay the hell out of my head, Keira!' resonated in my mind, over and over. I wasn't trying to peek into her thoughts, but she was blaring that at me!

That did it. I finally reached my breaking point with her and her attitude. I wasn't trying to read her mind, but stuff in there just came spilling out, for Pete's sake!

"Look, will you give me a break, Gwen?" I slipped the credit card back into my purse and scowled up at her.

She looked away, watching a couple struggle with a toddler who was in the middle of a tantrum, overtired from the day at Disney. She turned back and her face was a tight map of anger. "I can't, Keira! I...I just can't trust you anymore! My privacy is completely gone where you're concerned."

"I've been trying to stay out of your head! Honestly, I don't care what you did with Roy for the past couple of days! It would have been nice to have dinner with you guys but you didn't even ask me." I glared at her and then strode across the lobby and out into the bright sunshine.

Her hand gripped my arm spinning me around to face her. "Why? So you could read our thoughts? I'm entitled to my privacy, Keira. You don't own me, you know!"

My mouth fell open. She was sounding just like her asshat brother, with this 'owning' nonsense! I didn't ask for my mind reading abilities to accelerate at warp speed. The least she could do was have a little patience until I figured out how to manage it!

Before I could even sputter out a snarky reply, she continued, "I don't feel comfortable with you anymore. This is not working out for me."

"What? You're quitting?" I couldn't believe this woman! She was ready to bolt at the first real issue between us? It was that horrible brother! He was to blame for her sudden turn about.

Her hand rose flagging a taxi that was coming up the street. She glanced down at me. "Yes. I think it's for the best." Again that smirk on her face, "But why bother talking? You knew all this anyway! And that's the problem. Get the hell out of my head, Keira!"

It was like I'd been totally sucker punched. I'd known she was still mad and on the verge of quitting but she'd actually come right out and said it. "Fine! Have a nice life, Gwen! Roy will take you back to Kingston."

She was about to open the door of the yellow checkered cab but she paused and looked back at me. "What? You're not coming back with us?"

"If I thought it was any of your business, I'd tell you. But since it isn't..." I turned and stomped back into the hotel. The door of the cab banged shut and then it roared off.

I sighed and looked down. Alone again. The family with the toddler were just getting on the elevator. Family. I still had Mom and Dad. It was time to pay them a visit.

THIRTEEN

I booked my own flight to New York and let Roy fly Gwen back to Kingston. After landing in La Guardia, I flagged a cab to take me to my parents' home in Manhattan. I was still steamed about Gwen up and quitting on me, but I tried to put that aside. I hadn't seen my parents in a few months and this would be a nice surprise for them, me showing up out of the blue.

I climbed the steps to the brownstone and knocked on the door. As I waited for someone to come to the door, I felt even sorrier for myself. Even though I had my own home in Kingston, I'd grown up in this house and here I was knocking on the door like some kind of salesman.

It took forever for my mom to come to the door after I banged on it for the fourth time. When it opened her blonde hair which normally looked absolutely perfect was a total rat's nest and her lipstick was smeared. Her blue eyes flashed wide as her fingers clutched the sides of her satin, bathrobe tight.

Waitaminit. It was almost 5:00 pm. What was she doing in her bathrobe?

Oh no! Another big eeeew! She was as shocked as I was seeing her...especially when I'd interrupted her and Dad. My God! They were almost fifty! Shouldn't they be playing bridge with friends or even supervising at the restaurant they owned?

"Keira! What's wrong? Why are you here?" Mom's voice cracked a little and then she took a deep breath stepping back to finally let me in.

"Hi Mom." My face felt like a furnace as I walked inside and set my bag down. "Sorry, I should have called to let you know I was... uhhh..." My face got even hotter. "Sorry for interrupting?" My voice was high.

"Is that, Keira?" My dad's voice boomed down from the stairs above.

"Hey Dad!" I called up the stairs. I turned to my mom who looked as embarrassed as I felt. "I was coming back from Florida and thought...what the hell? I'll visit you. Bad timing I guess."

I turned and slid my arms out of my jacket. This mind reading shit was a curse sometimes!

"No Keira...it's just that—"

I stepped forward and gave her a quick hug. "Before you say anything else, you need to know something. I can read minds. Nana taught me about it before..." I looked down at the floor. "I don't have to touch you to know what's going on in your head."

Her eyes widened and her hand went to her throat. "Oh." Now it was her turn to flash fire engine red.

Well, this was becoming more embarrassing by the second. I huffed a sigh. "I need a drink. Maybe you should go get dressed and give Dad a head's up on this before he comes down."

Sitting in the living room sipping my gin, I turned my problem over in my head. How had Nana dealt with this? She'd had the ability and yet it never had caused her problems. God, I wish she had lived longer to teach me more. I didn't expect too much solid advice from Mom. The gene that gave me my talents had skipped her; she was as normal as rain.

When they entered the living room, Mom's hair had been finger combed and she was wearing pants and a silk top. Dad's face was flushed above his white golf shirt. He came over and took a seat next to me, leaning in to give me a quick kiss on the forehead.

"It's always good to see you, Keira." He smiled and patted my knee.

I took another sip of the drink, relishing the slow burn in my throat. I didn't want to read any of their thoughts right then. "Gwen and I were in Florida. There were a couple of spirits that needed a nudge to move on. Oh. And Gwen quit."

"What?" My mother took a seat across from me. "What happened? You two were as thick as thieves. She was a lovely girl."

Dad got up and turned to my mother, "Care for a drink, dear? I've got the feeling you're going to need one." When she nodded, he went to the small bar in the corner.

I took a deep breath and faced Mom. "It's this new skill of mine. I can read minds as easily as talking to you. She felt I was invading her privacy and she couldn't handle it."

Mom leaned forward and her eyes were icy. "Did you? Did you purposely invade her thoughts?"

"No. Well, not on purpose *all* the time. I can't help it if her thoughts spill over, believe me! Some thoughts I'd rather not know. Especially when it comes to her and her boyfriend." I ducked my head and looked at them. "There are some things I just *don't* wanna know, if you get my meaning."

Mom and Dad exchanged a look and their faces flushed a deep pink. It was Dad who spoke next. "But sometimes you peeked without her permission, right?"

I chewed my lip and nodded silently. "Yeah, but Dad, you got to understand, it's so easy to do; everyone's an open book around me." I sighed. "Sometimes I really have to focus, yeah; but other times their thoughts just leap out at me." I held my hands out palms up. "I don't know how to control this."

He stroked his chin. "There's got to be a way to turn this off. I know it's handy at times, but you have to respect other people's privacy too."

"Your father's right." She stared at Dad. "Richard? Is there anyone—"

I waved my hands. "Dad's not going to know. This is something I'm going to have to figure out on my own, I guess." I got up and poured another gin gimlet. It felt good to be home and able to talk to them at least about all this.

"Richard, I think it's time Keira knew, don't you?"

I spun around at my mother's voice. Knew what? And then it hit me like a rock. Mom was glaring at Dad, her thoughts focused on him being a....a Guardian! Just like Lawrence had been to Nana and Gwen to me. A back-up in this field, someone to sense when things were going south and could get you out of danger. Except with Gwen, she'd also acted as an amplifier to my power.

Dad nodded his head, cupping the drink in his hands. "Yeah. It's been a while but maybe I could make some calls. I don't like you doing this without a Guardian, Keira. But we've got to get you some help in controlling your abilities first."

I rolled my eyes and let out a loud exasperated sigh. "Another secret? All these years and this is the first I find out about you, Dad? It was bad enough finding out I had a grandmother I never knew about, and now this?" I huffed down onto the sofa. "This family! Honestly!"

Mom reached over and tapped my knee playfully. "It's not so bad. Lots of families have secrets. It's just that ours are....well, they're different."

"I'll say!" I polished off half of the drink.

"I knew your grandmother before I met your mother. She knew right away when she met me that I was gifted."

"But Dad, what kind of gift? I mean you don't have any of the abilities I have."

"The ability to sense danger, Keira. That was Lawrence's main job. That's what your grandmother saw. When she introduced me to your mom, it was love at first sight." He reached for Mom's hand and squeezed it, gazing into her eyes. "It worked out well. I have loved protecting your mother and..." He looked over at me, "...and there was you."

Okay. Everything was all hearts and flowers but that didn't help me much. I needed to meet with someone more like me. Someone who had abilities to match my own. Someone to *talk* to at least. "So you think you might be able to find someone? I've got to be able to manage this better."

My father rose and squeezed my shoulder on the way by. "I'll make some calls. And another thing...you can't just drop in unannounced anymore."

The flash of the two of them in bed made me rub my eyes with the heels of my hands. "Don't worry. I'll never do it again."

***

As we were clearing the dishes from dinner, Mom turned to me, "Are you staying very long?"

I snorted, but there was a smile on my face, "Why, are you trying to get rid of me again?"

She continued putting the plates in the dishwasher, "Not at all. I just thought you might like to get together with some of your friends while you're here." She straightened, "or maybe we could go shopping, take in a play?"

"You know, normally that would be great but to tell the truth, I'm pretty beat, Mom."

"Transition fatigue?" she asked.

"I never called it that, but yeah. After doing one of them, I'm pretty wrung out."

She nodded. "Yes, I remember that with your grandmother. She'd sleep for two days sometimes."

I nodded, and my chin began to tremble. "Yeah... and Gwen up and bailing on me..."

Before I could finish the sentence, Mom swept me into her arm and held me. She stroked the back of my head in that special way only she could do. It always made every boo-boo hurt less.

Dad came into the kitchen and rubbed his hands together briskly. "I just talked to an old friend of mine..." He glanced over at Mom and then cleared his throat, "...Jody Sheppard. She'd love to see you and it just so happens that she's free for a few days before she's off to Malaysia."

"*Jody!* Seriously, Richard?" Mom glared at him. "You couldn't come up with anyone else to help Keira?"

My gaze bounced between the two of them—Dad looking sheepish and Mom like she was ready to kill him. I held my breath. It was weird seeing them like this but this Jody character was a bone of contention. I kept myself from prying into their heads, despite dying to know the dish.

His arms crossed over his chest and his chin rose, "Susan! That was years and years ago! You can't honestly think I've got any feelings for Jody after all this time! She's good at this sort of thing. Even your mother had to admit that Jody is gifted. And on such short—"

"No! Anyone but her! That woman will wheedle her way into our lives and cause trouble." Mom turned to me, "I'm not trying to be difficult but the woman's a first class bitch. Your father and her were an item before he met me. And after we got together, she was always catty as anything. I can't see her being nice to you, Keira."

There was no way I was jumping into the fray. If the woman could help me in this mind reading stuff, I'd be all for meeting her but not at the cost of Mom flipping out. When Mom stormed off to go to the living room, I shrugged looking at Dad.

His fingers threaded through his hair and fisted, and he stared down at the floor. "I was only twenty-two when Jody and I were a thing. When I met Susan, I knew I'd been just biding my time."

"But Nana knew her?" I leaned against the counter, watching him.

"Yeah. Pamela was hosting a party and Jody and I crashed it. She'd heard about your grandmother and wanted to meet her. Jody was psychic and a little arrogant about that fact. She thought she'd put your grandmother in her place but the reverse happened. Not that Jody wasn't talented. Even Pamela admitted that." He poured a glass of water and stood still just holding it as he gazed off.

The emotion that pulsed from him took me unawares. I felt him picturing seeing Mom for the first time, her long blonde sweeping over her shoulders, and her big blue eyes meeting his told me everything I needed to know. Mom was jealous with absolutely no cause to feel that way. "C'mon. Let's join Mom. I know we can convince her. If this Jody is even half as good as Nana was, I think I'd like to meet her."

I paused in the hallway and turned to him, "Where does this Jody live? Is it far from here?"

He smiled. "Not far enough according to Susan, but I think being across the country in California does it. I haven't seen her in over twenty years, but thanks to Facebook, I was able to connect with her."

"Social media is great, isn't it?" I turned and went into the living room where Mom was sitting stiffly on the sofa, nursing a drink.

I took a seat next to her and held her hand. It was hard to believe that such a confident, attractive woman like her could be so jealous, picturing all kinds of scenes involving Dad and this Jody. "Mom, this gift of mine is a curse and a blessing. Dad couldn't hide his feelings from me anymore than you can. He's still nuts about you and Jody is ancient history, a memory. You don't have anything to fear."

She sniffed and took a sip of her drink. But I could feel her resolve weakening. She looked over at Dad. "Funny how you could get in touch with her just like that, after all this time."

He threw his hands in the air, and shook his head. "Oh my God, Susan! It's the twenty first century. The internet, Facebook! She could have been in Tibet for all I knew and I'd still find her pretty easily."

She looked over at me and her eyes narrowed, "But you'll stay here for a couple of days, right? I'd like to spend some time with you before you get together with your father's old flame!"

"Oh my God..." Dad muttered and strode to the sideboard

to pour a drink. "She probably weighs three hundred pounds and has thirteen cats, for all I know."

Okay. I'd let him away with that fib. The woman in his mind, the one whose profile he'd seen was still a knock out, but Mom didn't need to know that. I turned to her, "I want to stay for another couple days. I haven't seen you guys in a while. How about we turn on a movie and pretend it's like old times?"

Mom stood. "I'll make some popcorn." She looked at me and grinned. "And for you, we have a fresh melon in the fridge, and a bag of extra large marshmallows in the cupboard."

"Yum!" I stood up and headed to the kitchen with her. Marshmallows and melon—now *that's* comfort food.

FOURTEEN

Three days later, I arrived at Jody's home in Redondo Beach outside of L.A.. It was a stucco bungalow in a sub-division built in the 70's or so. I didn't expect to find her living in the everyday suburbs. If anything, I had assumed that just like my grandmother, she would have preferred something in the country with oodles of privacy.

I paid the driver and then walked up to her front door. Before I had a chance to ring the bell, the door opened and there she was, in all her flowery, silk wonder. She was wearing a brightly patterned red and yellow belted caftan and sleek sandals. Her deep blue eyes were rimmed with layers of mascara and her cheek bones were high and pronounced. "Keira?"

"Hi." I took the hand she extended and smiled. "Thanks for letting me see you." It was funny. There were no thoughts or feelings that emanated from her and I could only go by her warm and welcoming smile.

She pulled the door wider, "Nonsense! You're Richard's daughter! Of course, I would make time to see you! How is he? And your mother?" She spoke over her shoulder as she led the way through the hallway and into a large sunny family room.

"He's fine...well they both are. Busy with their restaurant." I gazed around, tugging the overnight bag higher on my shoulder. The place was simply furnished in earthy shades of colour, more South Western flavor than West Coast.

She swirled around to face me, the smile beaming in her eyes. "Have you had lunch yet? Can I get you something to drink?" She was around Mom and Dad's age, but looked ten years younger—her face was smooth and unlined and her neck was perfect. Since we were in L.A., it was just as likely she had some work done as it was she had great genes.

"Just water. Ice water if you have it." I took a seat on the suede sofa and set my bag down next to me. Floor to ceiling windows showed a small patio and garden area and the blue of the ocean in the distance. "You have a lovely home, Jody."

"Thanks! It's not much but it's all I need."

I nodded at the window. "With a view like that you don't need much more, that's for sure."

She stopped and turned for a moment. "You're right. I've been here for years and it hasn't gotten old."

"You're sure you're not hungry?"

"I had something on the plane." When I looked over at her, the image of a fresh green salad, red tomato wedges and slices of crisp cucumber flashed in my mind and my mouth began to water.

"Sure I can't get you something more substantial than the doughnut and coffee you had?" Her grin was infectious as she rocked back and forth on her feet.

"You sent me that image, right? But before that I couldn't read you. How'd you do that? Block me, I mean." I rose to my feet and at the nod of her head, I followed her into the kitchen.

"That's why you're here isn't it?" She held a glass to the spout on the fridge and then added a couple of ice cubes. "And yes, I did have some work done; a little nip, a little tuck. And you're right. Everyone out here does." She set the glass in front of me and then got the fresh salad from the fridge and some utensils. "Richard told me about your grandmother. I'm sorry to hear she's gone."

She took a seat at the table and looked across at me. "You *are* gifted. I could tell the minute you got out of the cab.

There's an aura of silver and blue around you."

I picked up the napkin and set it on my lap looking down for a moment. My eyes clouded. "Nana said the very same thing when we first met—the silver and blue aura."

Jody leaned forward, her hand reaching out for mine. "She's still watching over you, Keira. I know the work she did and what you continue to do, but she and I didn't agree on some things."

I lifted my head. "Oh? Like what?"

"Your grandmother thought The Veil needed to be protected and that once you crossed over, you stepped up to the next plane of existence. It's been my experience that The Veil isn't quite so rigid. There's still a strong connection to this plane, especially when it comes to people you love."

"You're saying she can come back? She can slide in and out of The Veil to be with me?"

She shook her head. "I don't know about coming back and forth through it. None of us really know what lies beyond after we die. I agree with you that transitioning souls trapped here is important work. But, as for what happens after that... well, I have a different opinion. From what I've experienced, I believe that we are still loved and watched over from beyond." She nodded her head sharply. "Pamela believed that once a spirit moves on, it's done with this world entirely; I think there's still some kind of connection."

"That's not much of a comfort to us on this plane," I said in a sullen voice.

"That's part of being human, Keira." She sat back and looked across at me steadily. "Let's get right to it, okay? From what your father said, you need to learn how to use your gifts more wisely, don't you?"

I nodded.

"Someone close to you has left you because of that, right? Gwen."

I nodded again and took a bite of the salad. "She felt I was invading her privacy. We were going to work together. She magnifies my power somehow and besides that, I like her." I wasn't angry with Gwen anymore. Over the last few days I put myself in her place and came to understand her point of view. She had every right to be upset.

She slapped the table and then got up to get a wine glass and white wine from the fridge. "Would you like a glass?"

"Sure." I wouldn't mind staying with Jody for a few days if she could give me tips on how to control my gifts. At the same time, I could understand Mom's feeling threatened by this woman. She was gorgeous, from the auburn curls to the dainty toenails painted a flamboyant red.

She glanced up at me as she poured wine into the glass in front of me. "Guard your thoughts, Keira. At one time, I would have gladly torn every hair on your mother's head off, but now...let's just say that things happen for a reason. I've had a good life that I don't regret." She laughed and moved over to pour her own glass. "That's not to say, I'd want to do lunch with Susan, but I also don't wish her any harm."

"That's good to know" I picked at the pieces of lettuce. "But how do I do that? Guard my thoughts? They just happen."

"Before any action, there's a thought. Even thoughts that don't cause action are still powerful. You can change the universe with your thoughts. Like a pebble tossed in the ocean, there are ripples that affect even the current on the other side of the world. But instead of it being an ocean, it's the universe." Her eyes were so solemn that I couldn't resist the quip.

"That's deep." I munched on the salad and grinned over at her.

"Smart ass, huh? Your grandmother will never be dead as long as you're around." She sat back and sighed. "First of all, you need to learn how to protect your own thoughts from people like me...people who have this ability."

"Which brings up another question...how many of us are there?" I took a sip of wine, watching her closely. Was there some kind of network that I hadn't discovered yet? It would be good to connect with them, if there were.

"There's no formal organization, but many of us know one another. I could introduce you to a few people I know...people who are credible with true gifts and abilities. God knows there are tons of charlatans and quacks who prey on people. And you are bound to stumble upon genuine psychics yourself." She smiled, "But I was talking about guarding your thoughts...first things first."

"Why do I have the feeling that this is going to involve work on my part?" I finished off the salad and got up to take the bowl to the sink.

"It's hard at first, but like anything, with practice it becomes second nature." She rose and nodded for me to follow her back into the living room. When she sprawled in the overstuffed leather chair from where I sat on the sofa, she continued, "Close your eyes and picture some kind of barrier surrounding your head. It can be a wall of steel, brick or even an energy field. It doesn't matter what you choose, as long as it's something that you feel secure behind.

I don't know why, but I thought of clouds. I pictured them, thick and white swirling over my forehead and the top of my head. The odd thought popped into my head—Gwen, would she really go back to work at the post office?—disturbed the image I conjured. It was hard to still my mind to maintain a focus on the barrier.

I tried deep breathing, stilling my body to keep the thoughts at bay. When Jody spoke again, I jerked in my seat.

"Now the hard part is maintaining this barrier while you go about your normal day. But for now, let's just try a simple test."

I could hear her set the glass on the table next to her and then lean forward, closer to me.

"Think of some random image, while also feeling your barrier stay in place. I'll try to see what you've imagined."

Blue hippos prancing in a line, like the ones in Fantasia flashed in my mind. Immediately I thought of Sean. That was the last time that an image like that had been in my head! Was he also gifted like Jody?

I heard her sigh. "The only thing that's coming through is a colour, blue to be exact."

When I looked over at her, her eyes were narrowed. "Was I close?"

"You were right about the colour." I smiled at this small accomplishment. She hadn't seen the animal so there was that.

She nodded. "Not bad for your first try. You really do have a strong gift. You just need discipline to practice." She grinned over at me. "See? I know that's something you've heard a lot and not just from your parents."

"You're right, of course." I looked down at the floor for a moment. "There was a guy I recently met who I couldn't get a reading on. When I tried, all I got was random, ridiculous images. Could he be gifted like me?"

"This is somehow tied in with Gwen isn't it? It's possible you met someone with similar gifts to yours, but there's no telling how strong they are. You do know that just about everyone alive has these gifts to one degree or another?"

"What? That's crazy."

"No, not at all. Just about everyone's able to ride a bicycle, right? But only a relatively few become professionals at it. Lots of people enjoy playing a musical instrument, but only a few are rock stars."

"Well that made sense if you look at it like that," I said, nodding.

She took another sip of her wine. "Let's try this a few more times before we go on to something else...like maybe how you can stop dipping into other people's thoughts. Now that's really important...for your own sanity as well as theirs."

***

By the time the sun was setting, casting shards of red and orange across the horizon, my head felt like it had been squeezed in a vise. Thankfully, I'd only had the one glass of wine or the headache would be blinding.

"Just one more lesson and then we break for the day. Hell, we've been working so hard that I haven't even showed you your room. I wish I didn't have to go out of the country in a couple of days. This has been interesting working with you."

"Yeah. I'm bushed but another part of me wants to push on, learn more while you're here." I stretched my arms over my head and tried to ease my muscles. "As far as dinner, why don't I take you out somewhere? It's the least I can do."

"You know something? That will work better with the next lesson. We'll be around other people and we can practice what you've learned about how to avoid breaking into their thoughts. I know just the place. Do you like Italian?" She rose and went over to where her cell phone sat charging.

"I love it." I got to my feet and stretched again. The head ache receded a little.

She slipped the phone into some hidden pocket of her loose flowing pants and ran her fingers through the tumble of dark curls. She paused at the mirror above the small table at the door and put a fresh layer of lipstick on. When she was done, a car horn sounded and she smiled at me.

"I know this driver. Gerry is an open book, but I'm not going to tell you his obsession. I want you to use your protective barrier again, but this time it's to keep you out of his head. And I'll know if you aren't successful, so don't try to fool me." She grabbed her purse and slung it over her shoulder.

"I wouldn't dream of it, Jody. First of all, I believe you. You'd bust me in a heartbeat if I tried to fake it. And second, I really do want to get better at this." I looked down the walkway to the curb where the taxi sat idling. A handsome, dark haired guy was peering at us. It occurred to me that Gerry and Jody were more to each other than a taxi service.

As we headed to the car, I was suddenly awash in a sense of foreboding. I stopped in my tracks and looked around me.

Jody stopped too. "Forget something?"

"No," I said. "I just had the oddest feeling, but it passed."

"You okay?"

"Yes, let's go." I *wasn't* okay, but I was going to keep it to myself.

FIFTEEN

I'd been right about Jody's relationship with Gerry. He'd joined us at the restaurant and then came in for drinks after he drove us home. And he was still there the next morning, judging from the low murmurs and muffled laughs in the room next to mine.

After emerging from the shower, I slipped into a light cotton dress and sandals. I could hear them leaving the bedroom, still laughing and flirting outrageously, promising to get together again before she left the country. I waited five minutes until the front door closed and the hallway became quieter. There was no way I wanted to intrude on their intimacy. I sighed. Even Jody, a middle aged woman was getting more in terms of a love life than I was.

When I left the room, she was still leaning against the door, with a smiling afterglow. "Oh. You're awake. I hope we didn't disturb your sleep." She pushed off from the doorjamb revealing a purple hickey on her neck. "I've know Gerry for years," she said.

I followed her into the kitchen. I was dying for a coffee.

The doorbell blared a few times, followed by a series of thuds. Jody looked over at me blankly. "Who in the world is that?" The thudding continued, growing louder. "I'm coming! I'm coming!" she called out as she rushed to the door.

As soon as she opened it, I heard a man's voice shouting "Where the HELL is Keira!"

I froze when I heard the voice. No. It couldn't be! Sean? What the hell? I hustled out to the door where he stood. He took his glare from Jody and stared at me with cold rage.

The last person on this planet I wanted to see was this asshat. Everything between Gwen and I was fine until he showed up. Now he was stalking me all the way out to the west coast?

"What are *you* doing here?" I said through gritted teeth. There was no answer in his head, all that was there was those infernal elephants romping across his brain.

"It's Gwen! She's gone!"

SIXTEEN

"Gone where?" I asked.

He did a face palm. "Oh you moron," he said quietly.

"Hey! Who you calling moron!" I elbowed past Jody, got right in his face and shoved him. "Who the hell do you think you are?"

He dropped his hand and looked down at me. I was going to knock him into tomorrow. His face slackened. "Oh shit, you really don't know do you?"

"KNOW WHAT?"

"She disappeared, Keira. She and Roy never came home. They vanished."

Like a popped balloon, all the anger at this asshat disappeared. I was bewildered. "Vanished? As in like gone?"

"Yeah. They never showed up at the plane. His co-pilot tried calling Roy with no luck, and they brought the aircraft back to their home base the next day." He shook his head from side to side. "We didn't know anything was wrong until the charter company called your lawyer Thompson. They were looking for Roy, because he didn't show up for work for three days." He glared at me. "You couldn't be bothered to answer your phone yesterday, so I called your parents and tracked you down here." He looked over at Jody. "You going to invite me in or what?"

She swung the door open. "Yes, of course."

He stepped around me, and marched right in. I followed him and Jody to the kitchen. All I was able to get from him was a sense of aching fear and white hot rage. I'm pretty sure the rage was for me.

Jody motioned to the furniture in the living room. "I'm Jody by the way, and this is my home."

"Yeah, I know," Sean said. He pointed at me. "Her parents told me where to go." He looked from her to me. "Don't you people check your phones?"

"Mine hasn't rung, I'm afraid," she said as we all sat down. "So please, tell us what's happened?"

I sat in the armchair. "She quit on me, Sean. The morning we left Florida, she told me she didn't want to work with me anymore."

"Can't blame her for that."

"Y'know something? If you hadn't been such a total bastard, she probably wouldn't have!"

"Easy, Keira," Jody said. "Let's all try to stay calm, okay?" She looked at me. "You left Florida three days ago, right?"

"Well, this morning marks the fourth day," I said.

"We found out all about this just yesterday," Sean said. "I tried calling the cops, but they blew me off. They figure that Roy and Gwen are on some romantic getaway or something."

Jody's eyebrows shot up. "Oh! Is that possible? Could they be?"

"No!" both Sean and I said it at the same time. "Gwen wouldn't do something like that without letting her dad know," I said.

I had cut asshat off before he could say anything, but he just nodded in agreement. "Yeah, she's not like that. She knows Dad would be worried." He looked over to me. "This

Roy guy seems pretty steady too. I only just met him once, but I didn't get the sense that he'd just chuck his job like that."

"No, Roy's not that way at all," I said. "I mean, Gwen's great and all…"

"Damn right!"

I huffed a sigh and kept on. "But neither of them are irresponsible."

"Unlike some people I know," Sean said in a low voice.

"Hey!" I started to get out of my chair, but was shushed back by Jody. "Sean, you have to control your temper. This isn't Keira's fault. She wasn't with them; she was at her parents' home and then here. She had nothing to do with what's happened to them."

"It's *my sister*, lady," he said through gritted teeth. He pointed at me. "And I'm positive that this kid's tied up in this one way or another."

I let his latest slag go because a feeling of urgency and dread nestled tight in my gut. If I didn't know Gwen so well, I would have loved it if she'd gone off somewhere romantic with Roy, but that wasn't her style. She'd gone missing. And from the sounds of it, not just her, but Roy as well. "This is not good," I said.

Asshat just sighed and shook his head. I jerked forward, but before I could come back on him again, Jody got to her feet and pointed at us.

"Enough! Both of you! This isn't helping Gwen or Roy. We need to figure out a plan here." She paced back and forth, her fingers steepling under her chin. "You need to find out if there was any sort of commotion at the airport. If they were taken, someone must have seen something odd." She looked over at Sean, "You've got a photo of her to show them?"

"Of course. But thousands of people pass through there every day. What are the odds that someone will remember her?"

I got to my feet. "Look! It's a start! What else have we got to go on? I'll hire a private eye…hell, a crowd of them if that's what it takes to find her! In the meantime, I'm booking a plane back to Florida. I can't just sit and wait here." Sean may have talked to the chartering service but they didn't know him. At least I'd done business with them. I got up and went into my bedroom to get my cell phone.

When I pulled it from my purse I sighed. I had put it on Airplane mode yesterday when I flew out of New York and had never set it back. I tapped the screen, and saw a bunch of calls from Gwen's dad and my parents.

I noticed there was also a single voicemail from an unknown name and number. I clicked the button and held the phone to my ear.

"Keira! It's Roy. I was told to pass on a message to you. If you want to see Gwen again, stop meddling in other people's affairs. They let me go to tell you this. Keira, they mean business. I'll call you back as soon as I can."

The voicemail ended and I stared at the phone. I went back to the living room. I looked at both of them.

"Gwen's not gone. She was *taken*."

SEVENTEEN

After I played the message to Sean and Jody we sat in a state of shock. Finally, he stood up. "I need to use the washroom."

When he left Jody leaned closer and her voice was low, "He doesn't know what you do, does he?"

I stared at her for a long moment, my mouth hanging open.

"Keira! Get your head together!" Jody glanced down the hall and leaned in. "Does Sean know about the work you and Gwen do?"

"Jody, in case you haven't noticed, Sean and I aren't that close, y'know? I haven't told him a damn thing." I took a deep breath. "But I'd bet a million bucks that Gwen's filled him in."

She nodded. "That makes sense. Because of what's happening, he has a right to know." She sighed. "I have to take this trip, Keira. It's been in the works for some time."

I looked up when Sean appeared once more. "I'm calling the police," I said.

He stared at me. "Really."

"Yes!" I booted my phone.

"You know something? You really aren't all that smart."

"What!"

"Which cops do we call, Einstein? The police in Florida? The ones here in Los Angeles? Or how about wherever the hell Roy is?" He ran his hands though his hair. "What we do is we wait until we hear back from Roy. Now that you have your phone *on*, you'll be able to actually *talk* to him." He shook his head again and flopped into a seat across from me. He took a deep breath. "Sorry about the crack about you being not smart. I've been awake for more than twenty four hours and I get cranky."

"And rude."

"I just apologized!" He shook his head. "Y'know, you're something else; I *told* Gwen that you didn't know what you were doing?"

"Oh! So you do know what I do!" I leaned forward at him. "Since when?"

"I knew you were weird from the first time you tried to read my mind." He held up his hand. "Don't even try to now, Keira—or I swear to God—"

"I'm NOT!" Good grief this asshat could get under my skin easier than a starving mosquito! "So you know about The Veil."

He snorted. "Yeah. Gwen told me about that stuff; ghosts and," he held his fingers up in quote marks, "*transitioning spirits* after you left the house. You—defender of the Universe. That's a laugh." He flipped his hands. "But, she told me the money was good; and she liked Roy…" He let out a huff of air. "She wouldn't listen when I tried to explain you two were in wayyy over your heads."

I gritted my teeth so hard they hurt. "It's *important* work, asshat. Lot more important than shuffling papers in some damn cubicle."

"Asshat? What the hell does that even mean?" He smiled at me in the most scornful, amused way. I felt my face burn.

Jody jumped to her feet. "Stop it! Both of you! You're acting like children!"

Before I could say another word, my phone rang. We all went still, staring at it. It was from an unknown caller and I pressed the button.

"Roy?" I said.

"Yes!"

"What the hell is going on?"

"Look—the battery's dying on this damn thing! I'm at an airport in Romania."

"Romania?"

"Yeah, Bucharest. That's where they took us. We got jumped at the car rental parking lot in Florida." He paused, sorrow in his voice. "We thought they were cops! They pulled guns and badges on us and got us into a car! Then they gave us both needles and knocked us out!"

"But—"

"Just listen! They're boarding my flight! I'm going to Ireland! Before they let me go to contact you, I heard two of them talking about going to Cork! Meet me in Cork, Ireland! That's where they're taking her!"

"Ireland?"

"Yes! County Cork! There's some castle or something there! I'll call you when I land! Look, Keira…" the connection started to get fuzzy and static-y.

"Roy! What's your phone number?"

His voice faded on and off as he gave it to me. I wrote it down. "Texting works too, Keira," he said. "This thing doesn't have voicemail, but texting works. Those guys…" his voice crackled and popped, and the line went dead.

"Roy!" I looked at my phone. 'Call Ended' showed on the screen. "I lost him." I looked around wild eyed. "We got to do something!"

Jody put her hand on my arm. "Did he say 'Romania'?"

"Yes! But now he says they're heading to Ireland!"

She nodded, her lips compressed. "Corruption. Romania's a haven for smugglers and human traffickers. They went there to get over to Europe. In Romania they could buy paperwork and whatever else they would need to get them into Ireland unnoticed."

Sean's voice was ice cold. "How the hell are you so familiar with this, lady?"

She turned to him, her face impassive. "Unlike you, sonny, I've lived a long life and all over the world." She took asshat down a peg without breaking into a sweat. Before he could say a word, she waved a hand at him dismissively and turned back to me. "I have contacts in Romania, Keira. I'm going to re-route my flight tomorrow and stop there and make inquiries on my way to Asia. If I learn anything, I'll contact you; keep your phone charged."

I nodded. "I'm going to Ireland."

Sean said, "Oh yeah? When?"

"Right now. You may think I'm stupid, asshat; but I'm loaded, okay?" So loaded I had an airplane charter service on speed dial. I hit the button for it and held the phone to my ear. While it connected, I said to him, "I'm chartering a plane, and you're coming."

"Try and stop me."

EIGHTEEN

Gwen

If she hadn't been so doped up by those thugs she would have sat up screaming. But she could barely move. She tried moving her arms and legs. They had her trussed up again with that damn duct tape. She was on her side, in the back of that van again, but now alone.

Everything was a haze from the time they were accosted at the rental return lot back in Florida.

***

An unmarked car, but with grill lights and a bubble on top had skidded up next to them. Two guys in cheap suits piled out of the car flashing guns and badges. Before they could say a word, they were handcuffed and thrown into the back of the car. Then the smaller of the two jabbed each of them with a syringe and watched her, licking his lips, as she passed out.

She didn't even know how many days had passed! When

they were both awake again they were chained by their feet in some store room. Some stale sandwiches, bottled water and a chamber pot behind a screen.

"Roy! What's happening to us? Where are we?"

"I think we're in Europe someplace, Gwen!" he whispered. "We were on a cargo plane. When we landed, I had come to and saw Cyrillic writing at the airport through one of the portholes."

"Europe! Why?"

"I don't know."

"What do they want? What should we do?"

A door flung open and the shorter of the two men strode in. "You'll be doing whatever we tell ya's!" He grabbed Roy and stuck him in the arm with another needle before Roy could make a move." Then he eyed Gwen. And licked his lips. As soon as Roy stopped struggling, he crept over to her.

"Please…" she curled up in a ball, knees to chin.

"Don't worry dearie, won't be but a pinch," he said, bending over.

Her feet rocketed up into his face smashing him backwards onto his ass.

He sat up. "Joe! Get in here!" The taller buffoon came through the door. "Hold the bitch down! Watch her now!"

He was a huge man but moved like a cat. Joe grabbed her like a rag doll and pinned her to the floor before she make a move. "I got 'er, Keith."

The smaller one jammed another syringe into her thigh and shoved the plunger home. Before everything faded, she saw the blood streaming from his face.

She passed out with a smile.

***

At least they didn't kill Roy. They were both awake when they stranded him on the side of a country road.

"Tell your bitch boss we'll be in touch!" was the last thing she heard Keith say to Roy as they pulled away. He leaned over the backseat and watched her. "One more trip for you, dearie."

"How's your head?"

He rubbed the side of his face. "Yah, ya got me good."

She was able to pin down the accent. "You're Australian."

"And so what if I was?"

"Coming up, Keith," Joe said from the driver's seat. She could see lights in the distance. "Should we put her back under now?"

"Nah. Wait' till we're inside the gates."

The van slowed its speed and made a wide arching turn. The low rumble of an engine that faded fast, told her they were at an airport. Her heart beat faster as she thought of what she could do to escape before getting on that plane.

When the van stopped, Keith spoke, "There they are. We're on." He got out and in a few seconds the double doors were thrown wide, letting some damp but fresher air into the cargo section where she lay.

"Bring it closer." This time it was Joe's voice. "Everything ready?"

She saw there was third guy and a gurney waiting outside the van. Joe's fingers closed around her ankle, hauling her out, and she let herself go limp, a dead weight. When her hips brushed the lip of the van, she let loose. Her knees bent and rose to kick into Joe while a scream rumbled in her throat.

"Shit! Get her, Keith! Don't just stand there!" Joe was holding his stomach bent over, while another set of hands grabbed her legs.

"I knew you'd screw it up!" Keith hauled back and the next thing Gwen saw was stars.

Her head bounced against the metal lip of the van and there was a blinding pain in her jaw, a coppery taste in her mouth.

The needle once more plunging into her thigh barely registered. She sank back, gasping for breath through bloodied nostrils. And then everything went black.

NINETEEN

Approaching Cork, night time in Ireland...

M s. Swanson?" a hand touched mine and I shot up straight in my seat.

The co-pilot of the plane was taken aback. "We're on our final approach, Ma'am. We'll be at Cork Airport in forty minutes."

"Oh. Thank you." He returned to the cockpit.

Sean blinked his eyes wide and shifted in the leather seat. "About time."

It had been a day from hell. Even though I told the charter company money was no object, for some strange reason putting together a trans-continental/*trans-Atlantic* flight together on short notice wasn't easy. They had to round up a rested crew, secure an aircraft and file a flight plan. We spent hours at the charter company office twiddling out respective thumbs and trying not to bite each other's head off.

We were both wrung out by the time we boarded, and both passed out as soon as we got to cruising altitude. Yeah, I'm that sort of a gal; I can sleep anywhere. I've fallen asleep on car trips with my parents, on the subway, and I've never been able to stay awake on airplanes.

By the time we took off, asshat had been awake for almost thirty hours. He was asleep before we leveled off, but was now looking around the cabin owlishly.

I got up and went forward in the plane to the small counter and fridge, taking out a bottle of water. I handed it to him. "Here. You look like you could use this."

He sighed. "Thanks." He took a long swallow, downing half of the bottle. He wiped his lips and turned to look out the window. "So we call the cops when we land?"

I shook my head. "No. We call Roy."

He spun his head to stare at me. "Are you completely crazy you moron? We need the cops!"

"No, asshat, I'm neither crazy nor an idiot." I couldn't believe how calm I felt despite his insults. Okay, okay, I woke up once during the flight to hit the washroom and he looked so damn perfect lying there sleeping I watched him for five minutes! Sue me. He was just as perfect asleep as he was awake, okay?

Until he opened his mouth and ruined the moment that is.

"Why the hell not?" he said, continuing in his asshatery.

I made my most condescending face I could. "Well, let's see…" I held a make-believe phone to my ear. "Hello, Irish Police Department? I'm Keira Swanson. I'm here with Asshat Jones to report a kidnapping." I paused. "Oh! Where did the kidnapping occur? In Florida, silly! They kidnapped Asshat's sister Gwen Jones and took her to Romania, but I have a reliable source that they've now taken her to Cork, Ireland." I paused. "Oh, I'm sorry—'County Cork'. My apologies. I'm an American who now lives in Canada." I furrowed my brow like I was hearing a question. "Excuse me, you want to know why? Why what, exactly? Why am I living in Canada? Why am I with someone named Asshat?" I made a small laugh. "Oh! Why did they kidnap Gwen! Of course! Well… they kidnapped Gwen because they want me to stop doing what it is that I do." I paused again. "Oh. That. Yes. Well, you see, what I do is transition spirits of the departed… you know, 'ghosts'… yes; I help them transition from this earthly plane of existence to the next realm. You see, if I don't do this, the Universe unravels." I widened my eyes. "Yes, I'll hold." I made like I was covering the phone and whispered to Asshat, "They're transferring my call to the men in the white suits! They'll be setting up my padded cell right away!"

He stared at me in silence.

"So, yeah, Asshat. No cops." I held out my make-believe phone. "You wanna talk to them maybe?"

He held up his hands in surrender. "Okay, okay. You got a point." He sat forward in his seat. "If you don't mind though, that's 'Mister Asshat', okay?" He hit me with the sweetest, most guileless smile I'd ever seen in my life.

I put down my air phone. "Only if you call me 'Ms. Moron'."

It was the best 30 seconds of the last week for me. Who was I kidding? Of the last YEAR. We sat staring at each other just like normal people. Who have something unspoken going on. I didn't dare try to peek into his head, this was fine just the way it was.

He nodded. He looked around the cabin. "Nice plane."

"Meh—" I waved my hand. "It's just a rental."

He pursed his lips and looked down. He closed his eyes and said in a low voice, "I tried to tell her not to get involved in this stuff. It's dangerous. I told her she could get hurt." And just like that, the moment we shared evaporated.

It came to me all at once. I leaned forward. "You have gifts like Gwen too, don't you? Except yours are stronger. You were able to block me when I tried to read your mind."

"Why do you think I didn't want Gwen involved with this? When I said I knew that she would be hurt, I really *knew*." *Spoiled little rich kid dabbling in dangerous things with hardly any thought to others.*

My eyes opened wider and I leaned closer from the seat across from him. I'd read that last thought loud and clear! But, he'd wanted me to. "For your information, my grandmother trained me. I've had some success in this and I didn't twist Gwen's arm, you know! As for the money, my Nana left it to me so I could continue her work!"

"If anything happens to her, I'll make you sorry you ever met her." He glared at me and then turned once more to gaze out the window, his fingers, clenching and unclenching in tight fists.

"Well, since you know so much, then surely you can see how she is and how this ends." Hmph! Gotcha! My chin rose and I smirked at him before nonchalantly inspecting my nails.

"Listen smartass, it doesn't work like that! I sensed something bad would come of Gwen's involvement with you. And I'm sensing something bad right now about my sister. They've hurt her." He scowled at me with narrow eyes. "No cops, I get that. So what now, Keira?"

"First thing, as soon as we land, we'll get hold of Roy and find out everything we can. Then we'll figure out the next step."

He sighed and said, "Do you think she's okay? Whoever took her probably has her tied up in the back of a truck or something. If someone has the money to hire a plane to abduct her, they probably have professionals who are hiding her. At least I hope they're hiding her...not dumping her body somewhere."

"Don't even think that! Gwen's alive. If they're trying to get to me, they need her alive. It's the only weapon they have that will get me to do what they want. Although, once we get her back, what's stopping me from continuing with the psychic work?" The whole thing made no sense. There was a piece I didn't know about...there had to be. And the worst case scenario, if they killed Gwen, all bets were off. Surely, they realized that. And *who*, exactly were 'they'?

His fingers threaded through his hair and he looked down. "Aside from Roy, do you know anyone in Ireland? I mean, someone who is involved in this psychic stuff?"

"I wish. If only my grandmother was alive. She'd be able to

point me in the right direction." I closed my eyes and said a silent prayer, '*If you're out there and able to help, Nana, I sure could use some direction here.*'

But nothing came to me.

"Wishes aren't going to help us, Keira." I opened my eyes to see him staring at me intently. He leaned forward. "So what we have right now is you, me and Roy when we find him; that's not good." He shook his head, turned away with a frown. "We don't know the area and we don't have any contacts. I *told* her getting caught up in this kind of bullshit was a bad idea." He pointed a finger at me. "This is all your fault!"

"*Bullshit?*"

He waved his hands at me dismissively.

"Look, we'll figure out what to do when we land. Until then, keep your temper." I stared out the window. He was right though. This really was all my fault.

***

I scurried down the steps, exiting the small jet. Sean was right on my heels, racing to the building. Once we'd cleared customs, and strode into the main section of the terminal.

"Okay, we're here. Now what, Einstein?"

I held up my finger and took my cell phone from my bag. "I'm going to try to contact Roy and see if he has any information" I punched the numbers into the phone and held my breath. Would my phone from the U.S. be able to call his phone from Romania while I was trying to place the call from Ireland? I heard it ring, then he answered. Wonders of modern technology.

"Hello Roy?"

"Keira!" He went on in a rush. "Last night a charted plane came in from Romania. There was a woman who was unloaded on a stretcher. An ambulance was waiting once they got through the rigmarole of Customs. It was a tall brunette on the stretcher. It had to be Gwen!"

I stared at Sean. "You found all that out?"

"Yeah, when I arrived, I asked around. Being a pilot myself

gave me a leg up in talking to people. I met a guy who saw it all go down. He's a pilot for Ryanair."

"What happened?" I pressed a button to put Roy on speaker so Sean could listen in.

"He was just leaving the airport when he spotted her being loaded into the ambulance. He got delayed, following behind it, which pissed him off because he had a short layover and wanted to get some sleep before the next day when he was scheduled again. He said it surprised him when the ambulance turned left onto N40 instead of heading into the city and one of the hospitals. It headed away from the city towards the coast."

"Where are you? Can we meet up with you?"

"I've been driving down the N40 asking at every gas station and store along the way if they saw the ambulance. I've made it to a town called Bantry."His voice hitched for a few moments, "Although it's like looking for a needle in a haystack. I'm driving in the right direction but they could be anywhere."

"Look, stay where you are. Sean and I will get a car and meet you."

"Okay. There's a pub here. I'll ask around. If I find anything out, I'll call."

I ended the call. I grabbed Sean by the arm. "C'mon—" We both stopped dead in our tracks when I touched him.

It was like a jolt of electricity going through my body. I could only stare up into his eyes, my mouth falling open. An image of Gwen, tied up in a dimly lit room flashed in my mind. It had been so clear yet was gone in an instant. When I touched him, it had been like with Gwen, but even more intense. Just like with her, I had felt a surge in my ability; able to see auras around people walking by and then that microscopic flash of Gwen.

"Did you feel that?" I said.

He pulled his arm away. "What the hell was that?"

"I think *that* is how we're going to find her, Asshat. Let's get a car and see if we can find someone to drive for us." I took the lead following the signs for 'Auto Rental'.

There was only one counter open with a guy about our age behind it. I fished my card from my purse, plopping it down in front of the young man at the counter. "We need to hire a car and driver. I'll pay whatever you want if you can take us west to some place called Bantry."

His head bobbed and he smiled. "Bantry? It's not far from my own flat. I'm off in about ten minutes if you'll wait." The guy's accent and dimpled smile were a welcome sight after Sean's scowls. For the first time since, Sean had barged into Jody's house, I felt my neck muscles release some of the tension.

"Sure. Just make sure it's a *big* car. We may be picking up a couple of passengers." Also, the seed of a plan had taken hold in my head.

He laughed and bent down under the counter and when his hand rose he held the keys, the fob showing the familiar Audi logo. "The Q7. I never thought I'd get the chance to drive it." He slid the paperwork in front of me and handed me a pen.

Sean stepped closer, "We might need it for a few days. Can you do that?" He leaned his elbows on the counter and sighed.

"You'll be wanting to hire me as your driver for a few days?" His eyes flitted from Sean to me. *'What in the world are these two up to?'* popped into my head. I couldn't help but chuckle. He thought Sean and I were a couple!

I leaned in. "We're trying to find his sister, my best friend," I said. "The last thing we've heard is she's in the area. Can you help?"

He looked at both of us again. *This could be an adventure! Better than this sodding job!*

"We'll pay you well," I said. "Very well."

"They pay me 400 Euros a week here."

"We'll be paying you that," I said. "A *day*."

He darted a look to Sean who nodded solemnly.

He extended his hand, and Sean, then I shook it. "Alistair Collins at your service." He looked around. "I'll be closing down now then. I'll phone my manager that I won't be in for a day or two."

101

Sean managed a weak smile, "I'm Sean and this is Keira. My sister's name is Gwen."

Alistair nodded. "And what brought your sister to the Emerald Isle?" He began printing off reports and locking up paperwork.

Sean and I darted a glance to one another. "It's complicated..." I said.

"Very well then," Alistair said. "Then we'll be off."

I nodded and then Sean and I stepped back. When my hand rose to rest on his arm, his head swivelled to look down at me. From the look in his eyes, he'd felt it too, the electrical current that passed between us when I touched him.

"We'll find her, Sean." This time, I felt empowered, rather than just mouthing the words.

When Alistair walked by, nodding his head for us to follow, Sean shrugged my hand away and stepped quickly to follow the young man who was sprinting ahead to the exit. On one level, I knew he was right that there was no time to lose but on another, I couldn't help the knot in my stomach at the anger that had flared in his eyes. The last thing he wanted was any contact with me, but he might have to submit to it, if we stood any chance of finding Gwen.

TWENTY

Gwen, early morning, Ireland...

At the loud bang, her eyes fluttered open. The vehicle stopped and the rear doors were thrust wide. When she tried to sit up, there was pressure on her chest, forcing her to fall back onto the mattress. A wide strap bit into her arms and chest, securing her to the gurney.

"She's awake." It was Joe, riding on the bench seat next to her.

"Let's get her in, so I can get this ambulance away from here. It's not the most inconspicuous way to travel although it did the trick at the airport." It was another guy with a thick Irish accent, reaching in to unlatch the brake on the gurney and yank it out of the vehicle.

Immediately Keith took a spot on the other side, sliding the stretcher out and onto a wheeled platform. Gwen tried to move her leg but the restraint at her knees held her still. Whatever they had given her made her head throb and stomach feel like she was going to throw up. Gwen could smell the salt water and odour of the sea and the air was damp and chilly on her skin. She was still in the light blouse and slacks she had been wearing in Florida; the ocean's chill went right through her bones.

"Is the big guy here?" Joe followed them as they wheeled Gwen across the pavement and up a long walkway.

She waited for Keith to answer Joe's question. But, it was the Irish guy who replied.

"That Mercedes over there doesn't belong to the maid, I'd venture." He chuckled and continued, "Soon as we get 'er inside, I'm off. I've no wish to see his Lordship if I don't have to...other than getting paid, that is."

From behind, Joe's voice quipped, "I'll be sure to tell Mr. Holmes you send your regards, Mike."

Immediately Keith whipped around, "Shut your gob, Joe! She's awake, remember?"

Holmes! Now, she had a name at least. She closed her eyes, feigning sleep once more in the hopes that they'd let something else slip. It's too bad they hadn't said the name when Roy was still there. She said a silent prayer, *'Please God, let him be okay. And send some help my way, while you're at it.'*

"Fat lot of good it'll do 'er. She's already collateral damage, in my opinion. Once the—"

"Shut the hell up!" Keith left the side of the stretched and she could hear a grunt, like Joe had just been punched or something.

Collateral damage? Any hope that she had of getting out of this alive were fading fast. This was about Keira. Once they lured Keira into their trap, they wouldn't need witnesses to tell the story. And if Keira was smart, she wouldn't come anywhere near this crew.

Her throat grew tight when she thought of her dad and Sean, home. Would she ever see them again?

As for Keira, if only she'd never met her! Keira. She thought of their last meeting and how angry she'd been about her snooping in her thoughts. If only she could snoop right now! She was by the sea, probably Ireland, if the guy helping,

Mike, was any indication. And this Holmes character...the name might mean something to Keira. It was a shot in the dark but at that point she'd try anything.

As they wheeled her into the stone house, Gwen repeated a mantra in her mind. *'Keira help! The coast of Ireland, Holmes has me captive!'*

When she was wheeled into a small room, rough fingers tore the restraining straps from her body. Her eyes opened to see an old man, with a huge, walrus moustache, narrow eyes behind thick glasses peering down at her. Keith and Joe were on the other side of the gurney, watching the old man. This had to be the boss—this Holmes guy.

"Do you need some water or food?" His voice was gravelly and low. He was stout, and his chest puffed out even farther when his hands clasped behind his back.

Joe reached over and ripped the duct tape from her mouth, sending new levels of pain through her bruised and beaten face.

She pushed herself higher, rolling the stiffness from her shoulders. "I need to use the bathroom." Even though she hadn't eaten anything or had even a drink of water in the last twenty four hours, the last time she'd been able to go to the toilet was equally as long.

The old guy looked over at the two other men and nodded. He turned and left the room, walking stiffly. From the way he carried himself, he was arthritic, which considering his age wasn't all that unusual.

She held her hands out and jerked them higher, waiting for the duct tape to be removed. Joe freed her wrists, then her feet.

"C'mon." Joe's hand gripped her arm, tugging her from the gurney. She struggled to keep her balance. He gripped her forearm like a steel trap, yanking her along until they had left the room and were in front of a closed wooden door. "There. No tricks or I'll give you what for." He turned the handle of the door and pushed it wide.

When she stepped in, there was a sink and toilet and nothing else. Not even a mirror, although she didn't need to see her face to know from the dull throb that her eye was black and cheek swollen. She finished but remained in the bathroom a few minutes longer, once more reciting her silent plea to Keira for help. Her eyes watered and she tenderly wiped the tracks from her cheeks. There was no way she was going to let that thug see her cry.

She opened the door and there he was, all six feet six of him, looming over her. She took a deep breath, "May I have some water, please." It galled her to be polite to that jerk, but it was probably the only way she'd get anywhere with him.

"In a minute. Back in the room with you." He shoved her back to the small room. She passed a window and sneaked a glance, reassured by the sight of the beach and blue water that she'd been right about being by the sea.

Keith turned from where he stood, "Take a seat." His head jerked to the side, indicating an upholstered, green leather chair.

She nodded and walked over to it and sat down. The door shut and Joe was gone when she looked across the room. It was probably useless to ask but she had to try. She looked at the cold cruelty in Keith's eyes, and her voice was soft, "Why am I here?"

"You'll find out soon enough. After you eat and have something to drink, the boss'll be back. If he thinks you should know, he'll tell you." His hips propped against the gurney and he looked over at her. He had the eyes of a dead fish.

"What about Roy? Did you hurt him?" That was the best she could hope for—that he wasn't dead, like soon she might be.

"No. He's alive. That's all I'll say." His eyes narrowed and he looked away for a moment. "If we wanted him dead, believe me, he would be." Why didn't they kill him? Oh yeah; so he could send a message to Keira.

Gwen's shoulders dropped and she let out a long sigh of relief. At least Roy was alive. There was another sliver of hope in all this.

The door opened and Joe strode in carrying a tray, propped

against his stomach. There was a plastic glass of water and a sandwich. He set it on her lap and then stood back watching her. All the while that Gwen ate, she looked down at the plastic tray, chanting her prayer for Keira's help.

'Keira help! The coast of Ireland, Holmes has me captive!'

TWENTY ONE

2:20 A.M., Ireland...

A half hour later, we were on the highway, heading away from the airport.

"You're paying me a fair bit to be your driver," Alistair said. "You'd be able to hire a taxi for half the money." He drummed his fingers on the steering wheel. "Your sister, Sean... is she a run-away?"

Sean grimaced. "No..." he looked over his shoulder at me.

The two of them were side by side in the front seat, and like a little girl, I was relegated to the back seat. It chafed the hell out of me, but I had kept my peace. I needed their help. There were bigger stakes than my wounded pride. And, to tell the truth, Sean just acknowledged my authority by not answering the question.

I sat up on the edge of my seat and leaned forward. During our time together I had gently probed Alistair. He was a good guy; pretty honest, kind to his Gran, and an older brother like Sean. And, like most guys in their mid-20's, he fantasised about being a man of daring, but never acted upon it.

"Alistair," I said, "we're pretty sure that Gwen was taken against her will."

"What? Why?" He put on the brakes and threw the car into park. "It's the drugs, isn't it? You two throwing money around like a couple of Hollywood stars, and now you're telling me this lass has been kidnapped?"

"It has nothing to do with drugs, dude," Sean said.

"Then what is it? Why haven't you notified the police?"

"Because..." I said, "it's very, very complicated. We can't go to the police."

"And why not?" He looked from Sean to me, and back to Sean.

"I..." shit. I didn't have a clue what to say.

Sean spoke up. "Look, dude; it's like this." He gestured at me with his thumb. "Keira's a big time heiress. She inherited a huge business and fortune from her Grandmother when the old lady croaked."

"Sean! That's my Nana!"

He rolled his eyes and looked at Alistair. "There are some people who think she's in over her head, being at the top of this business, and they're trying to pressure her."

"That sounds illegal to me. Why not the police then?"

Sean was on a roll. "Because if word got out that this was going on, the media would have a field day." He turned his hands out palms up. "They're trying to play a mind game with Keira, and we can't let them get away with it." He shrugged. "Right now, we don't have any proof. But once we do, we'll make sure that the cops are called if we need them."

Alistair looked straight ahead. "You're not telling me everything, are you?"

"Nope. We don't know you that well, man."

"I see." He cocked his head to the side and looked at me from the corner of his eye. "This can get dangerous, can't it?"

"Yes," I said. "But it's a greater danger if we do nothing."

He shook his head. "I must be daft," he said with a grin. "But it's an adventure. Let's get cracking then." He put the car back into drive and punched it. "Do you know what sort of car she's driving?"

"She's not driving. They took her in an ambulance," said Sean.

"Brilliant! I've got a few friends in Bantry. Bantry's not large, more like a small town than anything else." Alistair's profile, the small nose and puffy cheeks were highlighted by the dash lights of the SUV as well as oncoming traffic. He glanced over. "Chances are someone would have spotted an ambulance, that weren't local."

"We can only hope. When we get closer, I'll call our friend Roy. He was taken as well, but they dumped him." I stared at the highway ahead. It was time to tell Sean, my idea. This was going to be awkward with Alistair there. Already he was thinking of this adventure, like he'd stepped into some kind of Jack Reacher novel. Now I was going to amp that up to Stephen King weird and totally blow his mind.

"What the hell? They kidnapped *two* people? Who would do such a thing? Are they terrorists or something?"

"No. In a minute, I'll explain what I know." I turned from looking at Alistair to peering back at Sean. He was biting at a hang nail on his thumb but dropped his hand and our eyes met. "Sean. I need to touch your hand. I don't know what it is about you, but I know this will help me in locating Gwen."

I could feel Alistair's sharp swivel, peering at me while trying to keep the vehicle straight on the road, but I ignored him. It was the squint of Sean's eyes and the muscle twitching in his jaw I needed to focus on. I had to get past that iron barrier he held between us...not because I wanted to, but because we needed to if we were going to save Gwen.

"You felt it too when we touched at the airport—that surge of power, like electricity."

Beside him, Alistair muttered, "Now's not the time for romance, I'm thinking."

"Be quiet, Alistair." I turned back to Sean and extended my hand, resting my arm on the back of the seat.

"What do you think that will do? Remember it was your so-called gift that landed my sister in hot water." He rested his hands on his knees and sat back.

"Will you stop being an ass for just a minute? You want your sister back, don't you? Well, it's a big country and even with Roy's lead, we're still pretty much in the dark about finding her." I sighed. "I got a flash of her in my mind. Just a glimpse of her tied up in a dim room, when you touched me." I wiggled my fingers, pushing my hand as far as I could over the seat, almost touching him.

"What the hell are you talking about, love?" Alistair couldn't stop himself but I chose to ignore him.

Slowly, Sean's hand rose and his fingers closed around mine. The jolt of electricity sparked between us and surged through my body. I gasped and then took a deep breath, *"Gwen? Where are you?"* I closed my eyes, seeing her in my mind's eye, but it was her face as she was leaving me at the hotel in Naples. There was nothing else, aside from the red glow of anger about her. After a minute of this, I looked back at Sean and shook my head. "Nothing. She might be asleep. Honestly, *before* it was clear, but now...nothing." My gut sank like a stone and I looked away, even before he snatched his hand back.

"The great *Keira.* I should have known better." He stared out the side window and shook his head.

When I looked over at Alistair, his mouth had fallen open, stealing glances at me.

"I'm psychic, Alistair. I think Gwen sent me a message earlier and I wanted to try again. How much farther till Bantry? I might as well call Roy and let him know when we'll be there."

My fingers shook as I punched in the numbers on the cell phone. Time wasn't on my side. And Gwen wasn't communicating. Would we get there in time?

TWENTY TWO

W hen we pulled up to the gas station in Bantry, there was only one car parked there. It was close to four in the morning, so that wasn't surprising. I looked over and Roy was at the wheel of the small car, his head resting against the window. I got out and rapped gently on the glass.

His eyes flared open and the car door shot wide when he got out. "Keira!" It was only in the glow of the street lights that I noticed the cut on his forehead and dark moons under his bloodshot eyes.

"Roy." I folded my arms over his shoulders and hugged him. "I'm so sorry this happened." When I held him at arm's length, he sighed and his shoulders slumped lower.

Sean came up behind us and tapped Roy on the shoulder. "Gwen...how was she when you left her? If they hurt her...so help me, I'll kill them."

He looked at both of us wide eyed. "I called you yesterday! You haven't heard anything from them? That's weird. I figured they would have contacted you directly by now."

"No," I said. "There's nothing. My parents haven't heard anything, Mr. Thompson hasn't heard anything."

"My Dad hasn't had anyone contact him either," added Sean. "As far as he knows, you and Gwen are on a romantic getaway."

The two of them stared at each other silently.

"We didn't have a chance, man," Roy said. "They pulled up in a black sedan, jumped out and had us in handcuffs at gunpoint *fast*." He inhaled deeply. "As soon as they had us in the back seat, they jabbed us with some sort of drug." He looked away. "I couldn't do a damn thing; those guys were pros."

Sean put a hand on his shoulder. "I know, man. We'll fix this."

I spoke up. "Look, we've got to get some sleep. It's no good trying to keep driving when we don't have anything to go on. At least we know they were headed this way."

Sean nodded. "I hate to say it, but she's right. All of us need some shut eye." I looked over at Sean and my mouth fell open. He was actually agreeing with me for once?

Alistair moved closer to us and added, "There's a hotel just a few blocks away."

I tugged at Roy's arm, "C'mon. Ride with us. You need some sleep and a fresh start." The poor guy looked dazed and in no condition to be driving any kind of vehicle, especially in a foreign country on the wrong side of the road.

I glanced over at Roy before opening the door to the SUV. He sighed and his voice trailed off as he got into the back seat with Sean. "There were two of them, both Aussies."

Alistair started the car and we rolled down the sleepy street. I stared ahead, the buildings and storefronts barely registering in the morning light. Roy was right about this being odd. I had been expecting a call from Gwen's kidnappers too. Why hadn't they, if it was all about stopping me, then you'd think they would try to contact me.

The lights of a large, four story complex appeared. We were right on the coast and this hotel was nothing like the quaint Irish hostelry, I had pictured in my mind—it was exactly the opposite. It was as modern and large as anything you'd see in a major city. The car stopped outside the main entrance and I turned to Sean and Roy. "I'll get this. Four rooms in the quietest part of the hotel they have. We'll get together at ten in the dining room and go from there. If you need anything, a toothbrush, change of clothes, whatever, put it on my tab."

Alistair looked over at me and winked his eye. "This sure beats couch surfing at my buddy's flat."

***

A knock at my door, roused me from a fitful sleep. I hadn't even peeled the clothes from my body when I'd fallen into bed in what seemed like only a few hours before. I swear I was still running, being chased by some thug in my nightmare, when I jumped out of bed and raced to the door. Just in time, I remembered where I was and the fact that some unknown enemy was nearby. I yanked my hand back and asked who it was.

"It's Sean."

I opened the door a crack, not chancing removing the security lock. Sean stood there peering down at me, his eyes bloodshot above the dark shadow of beard growth. "I...um...I want to give it another try."

He didn't need to explain what he meant. He was as desperate for clues as I was, and if we could somehow make a connection with Gwen by joining hands, he was willing. I pulled the door wider and stepped back.

"Did you get any sleep at all?" I closed the door and stepped closer to him.

He shook his head and looked away. "Maybe a few minutes off and on. I kept thinking of Gwen...how scared she must be right now. I've got this feeling we're close to where she is. It was hard to just stay in the room when I wanted to just keep searching." He looked over at me and his eyes looked defeated. "So here I am."

My fingers threaded through the locks of hair hanging over my cheeks tugging them back. I looked up at him and took a deep breath. "Just so you know, I don't like this anymore than you do. I wish it were me that they'd taken instead of Gwen. But it wasn't."

"I'll second that. Gwen should be home with Dad, instead of caught up in some dangerous scheme with you." His head fell back and he looked at the ceiling letting out a long sigh. "And here I am, also getting sucked into your hocus pocus."

Despite the fact that I wanted to slap him, I held my hands out before me, waiting for him to grasp them. It seemed like forever but he slowly raised his hands to close his fingers over mine.

Again, it was like a light switch was thrown on, with everything around me taking on a brilliant intensity, the red drapes like fire, the soft cushiony mattress like the billows of a cloud. I could smell the hint of mint on Sean's breath from his toothpaste, hear his heart beat and blood pulse through his veins. We locked our gaze into each other's eyes and I noticed the silvery lines threading through his blue irises.

"Gwen." I said her name aloud, and it reverberated in the room. My eyes closed and I focused on her face.

I felt his grip grow tight when the image of her in a green chair, flashed in my mind's eye. *'Keira. The coast of Ireland. Holmes. Help me.'* It was a beacon that repeated softly with every beat of my heart. I opened my eyes and looked up at Sean. He'd heard it too! He'd taken down the barrier to me in his mind and Gwen's urgent plea was in his head and in his wide eyes!

"She's alive, Sean! And she's close." I squeezed his fingers in mine and for the first time the glimmer of hope I'd felt the other night grew stronger. She was on the coast of Ireland and....Holmes.

My eyes opened wide when I realized where I'd heard it. In the living room of my house in Kingston when Nana and I were talking...David Holmes, was my grandfather. But why would he use Gwen to threaten me, warning me to stop my spirit work? I was helping lost souls move on to the next level of existence...Why would he even care about that?

"What?" Sean jerked at my hands bringing my focus back. "What is this 'Homes' thing? What did she mean?"

I imagined the wall of clouds protecting my thoughts. He'd

be even more pissed when I told him the connection to me—not homes but Holmes, my grandfather who had kidnapped his sister. I made a snap decision to wait until I could tell him more. There was nothing to be gained with sharing this right now. Plus, he'd probably go off half cocked trying to find her on his own.

Before I could even come up with some story, there was another knock at the door, and Roy appeared.

"It's Alistair. He's on the phone with one of his friends who works for a parcel delivery service. He was on the road going north out of Bantry on Saturday morning and he saw an ambulance pass by. He only noticed it because the guy driving it was smoking a cigarette, and tossed the butt out. He thought it was kind of strange for someone carting a patient." Roy stood with his hands thrust deep in the pockets of his navy blue trousers, the white shirt of his pilot uniform wrinkled like he'd also slept in his clothes.

"That's it then! We head north. Let's go!" Sean brushed by Roy heading for the door.

I grabbed my purse and phone and looked over at Roy. "She's near the sea. We need to follow the coast line as closely as possible."

He held the door for me and then was right on my heels as we raced after Sean to the elevator. "Alistair's got the car out front."

"Well, he knows the area." When we got on the elevator, I put my hand on Roy's arm. "She's close, Roy. I wonder if we'd be better off splitting up again to cover more ground. We'll go get your car again and Alistair can go with you." I looked up at Sean. He nodded even though he looked like riding with me was the last thing he wanted to do.

My cell phone rang and I grabbed it from my purse. Jody! Maybe she'd heard something from one of her friends! "Hi Jody." My heart was going a mile a minute as I clutched the small phone to my ear.

"Keira! Where are you? Did you find her?"

Despite the sinking feeling in my chest at her words, I

answered, "Someplace called Bantry, in County Cork Ireland. Did you hear anything from your friends?" The elevator door slid open and Sean raced out and down the hallway to the reception area of the hotel. With him gone from earshot, I continued, "It's my grandfather, David Holmes. He took her, Jody."

There was a long pause and I started to wonder if the call had been dropped as I walked quickly, following Roy and Sean. "Hello?"

Finally she answered. "No, I haven't been able to find anything out from anyone. But why do you think it's David Holmes? He's dead. I met him only once, years ago at some party but I distinctly remember hearing he was killed in a plane crash."

I paused before going up to the reception desk to give them the room key and check out. "You're sure? Maybe it was another David Holmes. I think my grandmother would have mentioned it."

"Nope. It's the same one. Rich as sin, involved on the periphery with some Mediums and Psychics. That's how we came to be at the same party. But why on earth would you think he was involved?"

I looked over at the reception desk where Sean stood, thrumming his fingers on the hard surface. He scowled at me and then pointed to his wrist, signalling for me to hurry. "Look Jody, I've got to go. We're going to comb the coastline trying to find her."

"Be careful, Keira."

I clicked off the phone and hurried to the desk to sign the final bill that the freckled young redhead slid across the desk. Slapping the key card down I raced across the marble floor of the lobby and out the revolving door, Sean so close behind me that I could feel his breath on my neck.

The large dark Audi was parked, the motor idling with Alistair behind the wheel once more. I raced around the back and got in behind Alistair, glancing across at Sean, who was keeping his distance.

"Here." Roy handed a cardboard sleeve containing cups of coffee and a small brown bag to me and Sean. "It's not much but it'll have to do."

When I opened the bag the smell of cinnamon and vanilla wafted up. The buns were still warm! I hadn't eaten since breakfast at Jody's the day before. And who knew when we'd get a chance again? I looked around as we pulled out from the hotel and threaded our way through the streets to get Roy's car. What struck me most was the color of the high buildings, abutting each other. They ranged from red to yellow and green, while every so often a glimpse of the countryside and ocean peeked through. Another time, it would be fun to explore but right now, the only discovery to be made was where Gwen was being held.

The car slowed and pulled into the gas station where Roy's rental, a compact Toyota sat at the side of the lot. Alistair turned in his seat and looked at Sean and I, "We'll take the N71 as far as Donemark. It was just a bit north of there that my friend noticed the ambulance, although we're still not sure it was them. We can stop at the odd place and ask around. You do businesses and we'll try houses."

It was like finding a needle in a haystack but it was all we had.

"All right then. We'll stay in touch." Alistair turned and got out of the Audi. He looked back at me and winked. "Sure you wouldn't rather stick with me and let these two travel together?"

I shook my head. "No, you drive Roy's car and I'll be right behind you." I moved over behind the wheel.

All the while I watched Alistair drive back onto the street in the Toyota. "I have to tell you something, Sean." I swallowed hard but it was time to come clean with the other piece of the puzzle.

"The man who is behind this is named David Holmes. He'd be in his late seventies or early eighties, I think. If we're lucky, he owns property around here. We may be able to track it down if he owns any."

"So it's a name... nothing to do with houses."

"Yes."

"How do you know all this?"

I looked up at the traffic light and gritted my teeth. "I just do, okay?" Ahead, Alistair flicked his right turn signal on and when the light changed, he turned right.

"There's more you're not telling me. Who is this guy? Do you know him?" His hands flew up in the air and he shook his head. "Keira! For God's sake, he's got my sister!"

"I don't know for sure that he does....but my grandmother mentioned that name. I've never met him." There. I wasn't lying but if he knew the truth, he'd probably kill me. Just one more way that I was connected to the danger Gwen was in. Plus, we might need to try to communicate together, holding hands. Fat chance of that if his hands were around my throat.

"Fine!" His eyes closed and he huffed a fast sigh.

My hands were shaking a little but I managed to drive the car, focussing on Roy's rental up ahead. After a couple more turns we were on the N71 highway heading north. It wasn't like an interstate but more like a secondary road skirting businesses and subdivisions.

After a few miles the scene we passed transformed to more open country, with green pastures and farms. All the while the silence in the car was deafening. Sean looked like a ticking time bomb and I didn't dare to say a word. Finally I couldn't stand it anymore. He wasn't the only one worried about Gwen and he was acting like it was my entire fault.

Just as I was about to suggest we join hands to see if we could summon up any clue from Gwen, my phone rang, making me jump out of my skin. It rang again and my stomach tightened. This was the call I'd been waiting for. I slid the phone from my purse and glanced at the screen. 'Unknown Caller'.

I clicked the button and before I even had a chance to process my thoughts, it just blurted out of my mouth. "Hello, Grandfather."

TWENTY THREE

Sunday morning, Gwen...

The shrieks of sea gulls outside the window pierced her dreams, bringing the pain of consciousness. Her chest was heavy from the wide band restraining her to the narrow gurney, and her fingers were numb resting at her sides.

A dull grainy light filtered through the curtains, revealing the same drab room with the wood panelling and the green leather chair. She was alone and judging by the light, she knew it was early, probably eight or nine. Much as she wanted to go to the bathroom, she put the thought out of her mind. The less contact she had with those thugs the better.

They'd been in and out at different times the day before, leaving her mostly alone and tied up. The old guy, the Holmes character had only been there for a little while, questioning her about Keira. He wanted to know why...why a young woman would chose to work with spirits when she could do just about anything else in the world. It was like he was trying to get a line on her, find out what it would take to get her to stop. But there was more that he wasn't saying.

All the while he'd been talking, Gwen couldn't help getting the impression that he was in awe of Keira's power. He didn't say it, but she could tell, his mind was working trying to find a way to turn Keira...to get her working for him. As if! If that's what he wanted he sure wasn't scoring any points kidnapping her partner. But that didn't make any sense! What would he have her doing?

But time was passing by. She had to try the mind message again. It was the only thing she had to hope for, that somehow Keira's abilities would be strong enough to somehow pick up on her message. She closed her eyes and concentrated as hard as she could, picturing Keira and herself holding hands, while the familiar words shouted in her brain.

At the fourth round of the mantra-like words, her breath hitched in her throat and her eyes flew open. Sean? Somehow, he and Keira were linked. And unlike the other times where she felt a vacuum, this first time she got the clear impression that someone was picking up on her message. Encouraged, her focus narrowed and the voice in her head became louder still. *'Keira! Ireland by the sea. Holmes. Help!'*

But she couldn't help the vision of Sean that kept niggling at the edge of her mind. How many times when they were growing up had her big brother come to her rescue? Her chest fell remembering when she entered high school. Head and shoulders high above her girlfriends and most of the guys, she'd often felt like the cruel name the meaner kids had given her—Gwen-zilla.

But Sean had saved her that day, pinning Billy Mullins the bully against the metal lockers when he'd teased her. Billy's minions had fled like the cockroaches they were. But no one dared to call her that name again.

It only made sense that Sean would be searching for her. The surprising thing was that he was with Keira. He'd made no bones about the fact that he disliked her and hated the idea of their working together. It looked like he'd been right about that.

She took a deep breath to clear her head and resume her silent cries for help, but the door opened, banging against the wall behind it.

"Wake up!" Joe walked into the room and his fingers yanked the wide band undoing the clasp, freeing her chest and shoulders.

Her eyes narrowed watching him work at the strap holding her knees down on the stretcher. "I need to use the bathroom again."

Her hands rose and she rubbed at her wrists, trying to get the circulation flowing again. It was so tempting to lash out and punch the side of Joe's head. She might be able to daze him enough to run out of the room but then what? Keith was probably just outside the room and he'd get her before she had a chance to get out the door.

"Personally, I couldn't care less if you pissed yourself, but the boss wants to see you later. It wouldn't do to have you soiling his Lordship's furniture." Joe flipped the strap off and then yanked her arm, tugging her off the bed.

She could barely walk with feet like pincushions where a million needles tingled sharply. But she managed to get through the door while Joe's sour breath was warm on her neck, shadowing her. Keith was standing off to the side, and he glanced up at her before returning to scan the screen of his cell phone. As she walked to the small bathroom, her eyes flitted over the entrance, looking for any clue as to where she was. A name, an envelope, anything!

When she closed the door behind her, her shoulders sank and she gave way to tears. She'd seen nothing and the house was deadly quiet. This cat and mouse game wouldn't go on much longer before something really bad happened. She knew it in her bones.

Her father's face in her mind brought fresh tears to her eyes. How would he cope if he lost her too? Would she ever see him again? She buried her face in her hands as she sat on the cold toilet seat. Her mother. Maybe she'd be joining her in the afterlife instead of hugging her dad again.

"Oh Sean...Keira, if you are anywhere near here, please help me." It was a whisper followed by wracking shoulders as her sobs overtook her. It must have been a while that she just stayed there, her heart breaking at the bleakness of her situation.

The sharp thuds on the door were followed by Joe's snarly voice, "Did you fall in? Hurry up!"

She got to her feet and turned the faucet on, splashing her hands and face with cold water. She sniffed and then grabbed some tissue to blow her nose. Taking a few deep breaths to steady herself once more, she opened the door and stepped out.

There was only Joe there and his rough hand reaching for her arm to escort her back to the room. Quick as lightening, her elbow shot across catching him in the throat. His eyes bulged and his hand cupped his throat as he bent forward! Her knee jerked up, landing a hard blow at the base of his nose. She could hear the crunch of bones splintering as she darted across to the door.

Her feet flew down the granite steps. A long dirt driveway was bordered by fields of green. There was a stand of trees to the right. If she could just make it that far before the others were alerted she'd get away!

TWENTY FOUR

There was long pause before Holmes spoke. "Oh my, well done, Keira. I didn't expect you to be this insightful so quickly." He paused again and then chuckled. "You're better than I would have ever guessed."

Hmph! This horrible excuse for a human being had kidnapped my best friend and now had the audacity to try flattery. As if...

"Hang on." My voice was cold. I looked over and my gaze locked for a moment with Sean's wide eyes. I wheeled the car over to the shoulder and hit the brakes and before clicking the speaker button. It couldn't be avoided anymore. Anything David Holmes had to say, Sean should hear as well.

"Where is she? Let me talk to Gwen." When I said his sister's name, Sean jerked forward, the puzzlement giving way to a hard, icy stare at me.

"Not so fast. There's something I want from you, first." His voice oozed with a cold confidence. "You got my message from the pilot, did you not?"

"Yeah. I got it."

"If you hurt Gwen, so help me God, I'll make you wish you were never born!" Sean broke in, unable to contain the rage in his body. He glared at the phone while the muscle in his jaw tightened into a steel cable.

"Ah...I see you're not alone." Again the easy confidence in my grandfather's voice made my skin crawl.

"What did you think? That her family wouldn't notice she was missing? And that's not all, we've called the police. They have your name and there's an arrest warrant for you. You might as well, hand her over." I looked at Sean who was flexing his fingers and making hard fists. Sure, I was lying through my teeth; what could he do, sue me?

When silence met my words for a few moments I asked, "Hello? Did you hear what I said? Just tell us where she is. I don't care about anything else. Take off, leave the country but tell me where Gwen is now."

"Hmph. The police will never find me. Ever hear of numbered companies? But I am curious how you knew it was me."

"That's for me to know and you to find out." It was childish but it was all I could think of in the blinding rage consuming me. "Put her on the phone, if you want to see me. I won't agree to any of your demands until I know she's okay."

"It seems to me that you're not in any position to make deals, not with my bargaining chip."

"My sister isn't a thing, you sack of shit!" If David Holmes had been in the car, Sean would have torn him apart with his bare hands.

"Temper, temper. But very well. I'll put her on; but then Keira, you'll do as I ask. Hold on for a minute." His voice was oily and then dead air followed.

I looked over at Sean. "I never met him. My grandmother told me he was a bad character. But whatever he wants me to do; I'll do it, if it will get Gwen back. I'm so sorry, Sean." His stony silence made my heart ache...not just for him but for Gwen as well.

A noise from the phone, interrupted my thoughts.

"I've changed my mind. You don't get to talk to the girl yet. If you want to see her alive, you'll meet me in Targariff. There's a point of land, at the end of Shoals Point Road...that's where she'll be. Come alone. If I see anyone else, any police or anyone at all, your Gwen will pay the price of my wrath. Be there at three o'clock. Just you. Understand?"

"I'll be there. Just. Don't. Hurt. Her." The phone clicked off. My eyes closed and I had to fight the tears that stung behind them. I was in a helpless rage and absolutely terrified for what this man was capable of. Even through the telephone I could feel the blackness of his soul.

"I'm coming with you." Sean picked up his phone and his fingers flew over the tiny keyboard.

"You heard what he said! You can't or Gwen dies!" My nerves were as taut as a piano wire and now wasn't the time for him to be pig-headed. It was his sister's life, for God's sakes!

I looked down at the phone in his hand. God, if he was calling the police, so help me, I'd swat him. "What are you doing?"

"I'm locating this place Targariff on the map and Shoals Point Road and then I'm going to call Alistair and Roy. We've got a few hours to figure out a plan and Alistair knows this area better than us. Plus if this doesn't work, we'll want someone to know and inform the police. But you're right. Bringing in the police is way too risky for Gwen."

There was something niggling at the back of my mind. When David Holmes had come back on the line, his tone had changed.

I turned to Sean. "Something funny's going on here. He said he'd put her on the phone, but came back and refused."

Sean looked off to the side thinking. "What does that mean?"

"Why did he change his mind about putting Gwen on the phone?" I reached out and took Sean's hand in mine. The shock of it plus the energy surging between us yanked his attention from the phone. He stared at me and we both heard it in our heads. *"HELP ME, KEIRA! SEAN! THEY'RE*

COMING AFTER ME!" The contact was so vivid that for a moment I could see her, running through a copse of trees, hear the ocean surf in the background along with a car whizzing by her.

Her cries and pleas faded. "She's alive, Sean! She got away from them!"

"Where is she?"

We grasped hands again, and I called out to her, but got no response. "I think she's in that area where Holmes is at."

I froze when it dawned on me. My Spidey sense was red lining "Holmes doesn't know that we know that Gwen's gone. That gives us an advantage."

I wheeled the car back onto the highway and punched it. "Call Alistair and Roy. Find out where they are now and we'll meet up with them." I darted a quick glance at him. "I'm still going in there alone, Sean." There was still a few hours before I was supposed to meet Holmes. Maybe we'd surprise them be showing up ahead of time. Plus, if Gwen was out there, there was a chance we'd find her first.

TWENTY FIVE

Gwen...

She kept low, hurrying from tree to tree. Her legs trembled from the effort and she tried not to think of Joe slumping to the floor after taking the knee to his nose. She hit him hard enough to shove it right into his brain. Oh God! She'd probably killed him. It was self defence; he kidnapped her! God knows what else he had planned for her! She gulped and tried to shake it off; surprised at how easy she was able to.

Focus Gwen, focus! She was well away from the house before she heard the door bang and footsteps. Who else could be there besides Keith and that old guy? He had a bigger organization than just those two for sure. She'd have to stay low making her way to the highway. She could hear the sound of traffic and kept heading in that direction. Someone would surely help her if she made it as far as the main road.

At the crack of a branch, she looked back. Oh shit, it was Keith, looking right at her from a hundred yards back. She took a deep breath and dodged around another tree. He was in his forties and besides that he was a smoker. She might be able to outrun him if it came to it, but what if he had a gun?

Don't think that, Gwen! There was an open area just ahead and she'd have to leave the cover of the trees. Please Lord, let her make it across to the next crop of trees. She had to be getting close to the road.

There was a loud curse followed by the crashing of more branches. She took a quick look back to see him floundering to his feet. She darted out from the trees, using this small sliver of hope. Every footfall, she imagined a bullet catching her between her shoulder blades. Her lungs were bursting, gulping air as she sprinted like the Devil was after her.

'Sean! Keira! Please be near here! Find me!' At a break in the forest, she caught a glimpse of the dark pavement of the highway. She was almost there! The buzz of a vehicle coming from the left caught her attention.

She sprinted to the highway and stood in the middle of the road, waving her arms at the dark SUV. "Help!" She waved frantically, jumping up and down as it slowed. Thank God! She glanced back but there was no sign of Keith. Hurry!

The car stopped and she saw a dark haired woman behind the wheel, staring at her with wide eyes. She tugged the door open and almost fell into the car. "Please! Help me! There's a man chasing me!" Pulling herself upright into the seat she banged the door shut. Still, no sign of Keith yet.

"Hurry! Drive!"

The woman nodded and pressed the accelerator. She looked over at Gwen and then her hand slid to her door. Every lock in the vehicle clicked, locking the doors. "You're Gwen, aren't you?"

Gwen stared at her, still trying to catch her breath. "Yes. How did you know?"

The woman's face relaxed and she glanced in the rear view mirror, "I'm Jody. Keira's looking for you."

Oh thank God!

TWENTY SIX

T here they are." Sean pointed ahead.

Roy's rental was parked in front of a diner and Alistair leaned against the driver's door. I parked beside them and got out.

Alistair's rushed forward, fairly bouncing with excitement "You found her! I mean, we know where she is! I've hiked with friends near that point of land. It's not far."

Without warning my head swam and my hand clutched the hood of the car to keep from stumbling. I was seeing double and my knees went weak. Sean grabbed me by the waist just as my legs gave out.

"Keira! Are you all right?"Sean's words were far off, like they were coming from the end of a tunnel.

Something was wrong! But, the image of a wall filled my mind, preventing me from seeing anything beyond. Before, when Sean and I had touched, I'd seen Gwen, practically went inside her body as she ran through a forest. But now nothing.

"Look, we've got three hours till you're due there. Let's figure out our next move." Roy moved to the other side of me and helped walk me into the small restaurant. I was in a daze and let them lead me along.

At the table, Alistair and Roy were huddled over his cell phone, looking at a map, their voices barely registering as they scoured the screen, talking softly, making a plan.

"Drink this." Sean held a glass of water up, peering at me closely. "Just breathe, Keira." His other hand rose to rest on my back, and began stroking it.

Oh boy.

His hand made a pressure on my back, just like any other hand would. As he stroked it though, a sensation beyond the physical infused into me. I turned, staring at him. His eyes watching me took on a hue, a glimmer I never saw before. He kept his lips closed and nodded just so slightly as strength came into me, spreading though me like a breaking dawn.

"What are you doing?" I said in a whisper.

"Shhh..." He bit the inside of his lip and took his hand away. The pressure of his hand was gone, but the sense of well being remained.

"What the hell was that?" I said.

He made a small smile and looked away. "Would you believe an old Yoga thing I picked up?"

"No."

He shrugged and reached over and tapped Roy's shoulder. "Got anything, bro?"

"Alistair's got an idea." He nudged the Irishman. "Tell 'em."

Alistair was excited as a kid at Christmas. "There're lots of trees bordering the building, see that?" "We can sneak through the forest and surround the place, while Keira goes to the door." He looked over at me, "But mind you don't go inside. We won't be able to help you if you do."

"Let's get a move on," I said.

Sean nodded. "I agree with Keira. I say we go now. He turned to me, "You're good to go now, right?"

As if he didn't know what he just did to me. I didn't have a clue what it was, but he sure knew.

I decided to keep my mouth shut about that back rub; we'd keep it between us for now. So I nodded and gulped the rest of the water down. "I'm okay. Let's go."

"I'll drive this time," he said.

Alistair patted my shoulder before walking out the door to his car. "Follow me. I'll park half a kilometre before the road going down to the point. Keira, you're on your own from there. Just give us fifteen minutes head start before you start down that road." He and Roy headed for their car.

When Sean and I got into the Audi, he turned to me. "What came over you just now?"

"I guess I just had a case of the vapors," I said.

"Does that happen to you a lot?"

"No." My eyes widened. "Not since I was at Nana's!" I stared at Sean. "Oh boy."

"What?"

"When I first went to stay with my Nana... Every time... Every. Time. My... *powers* were about to expand, I felt that happen."

He snorted. "Your *powers*? What are you, Wonder Woman?"

That did it. I punched him in the shoulder. Hard. He let out a yelp. "Yes, my *powers* you idiot! As if you didn't know! Oooh! You are such a pain in the ass!" I clenched my fists. "They're some kind of mystical abilities that I don't even understand, okay? But every time they get stronger, I get hit with a dizzy spell like that!"

He stared at me in silence.

"And furthermore, Asshat, don't try to tell me that was some Yoga crap you did back there, okay?"

His face went blank and he started the car without saying a word.

Fine!

***

Roy's car pulled off into a side lane and Sean pulled in behind it. He turned the car off and then looked over at me.

"You're sure you can do this?"

Okay, we were calling some kind of truce or something. I took his hand. "I have to at least try. She wouldn't be in this mess if not for me." My hand was on the door handle and I turned to get out of the car and join Roy and Alistair. They looked like they were itching to take off into the forest that bordered the road.

Like a Knight Errant, Roy was on a mission to save his beloved. He was bouncing on his toes and humming to get this going.

Alistair was still acting like he was in a James Bond action film. "Remember. Fifteen minutes. It's not that far and we should be there by then." His fingers curled and uncurled and he too started to bounce on the balls of his feet.

Once more, Sean surprised me when his hand squeezed my shoulder. Another of those pulses of sublime comfort and strength flowed into me. "Be careful." With that, he was gone, sprinting after Roy and Alistair. In a few moments they'd disappeared in the forest, like Ninja.

I got back into the car and grabbed my phone. It was almost noon, only a half hour after we'd got the call from Holmes. So much had happened that it was surreal. I set the timer for fifteen minutes and then sat back in the seat, taking deep breaths.

Stop interfering in other people's affairs! That had been the message from my grandfather. He wanted me to stop my work with The Veil. But I was sure there was more than that. He had something else up his sleeve.

TWENTY SEVEN

The cell phone's alarm chimed. The fifteen minutes were up.

I squared my shoulders and started the engine. This was it. But the unease I'd experienced before had vanished. It was like I was in a dream. On one level it was my hands steering the car, flipping the turn signal when I came to the road, there was a calm clarity in my head—my nose picking up the scent of the sea, the evergreens, the sound of birds twittering in the trees, the colours sharp and vivid. Even the feel of the leather bound steering wheel, soft with a grainy richness swept through me.

And yet, I was also observing myself, driving the Audi down the narrow dirt lane. The stone house was just up ahead. Again, my vision filled with the grassy area surrounding the house and the copse of trees on either side. There was no sign of my friends but I knew they were there, hidden from sight.

I turned off the engine and sat there for a moment, trying to get a sense of Gwen, but once more a wall separated us. It was no mystery who was causing that to be. Now that I was here, the stillness of the place was unsettling. There were no parked cars nor movement inside.

Something was wrong.

I leaned on the horn, blasting through the silence. If there was anyone there, that would get them to step outside. My jaw clenched as I gazed at the door and then the windows, watching for any movement. After a few seconds of the deafening noise, I got out of the car.

There was no one there. Even though we were earlier than the appointed time, they'd already left. I didn't need to be prescient to know that.

Sean and Alistair appeared at the edge of the lawn, standing and watching me. Roy appeared from a area closer to the shoreline.

I walked up to the door and banged hard on it. "Gwen! Hey Holmes, if you're here, let me in!" When there was no answer, I tried turning the doorknob but it was locked tight.

Sean stepped up beside me and with a sharp jab, his elbow smashed the glass side panel of the entry. "I'm tired of dancing to this maniac Holmes' tune." His hand carefully navigated past the shards of glass and hooked around to unlock the door.

He threw the door wide open. When I stepped in after him, Roy and Alistair were right behind me. It was dim inside with the only light source, a window down the hallway. I made my way over to a small room and stepped inside. There was a stretcher and a green chair just like in my vision. When I touched the bed, the terror that Gwen had felt rushed through me. Not just terror but pain. It was then that I spotted the circle of rust coloured blood near the pillow. What the hell had they done to her?

"Keira!" Sean's voice came from further down the hall.

I hurried after him, to find a room lined with shelves of books and a large wooden desk set near a fireplace. Sean held an envelope in his hand and extended it to me. "It's got your name on it."

My fingers flew tearing the velum paper and sliding the note out. But that wasn't the only thing that fell out. I gasped when the thick lock of chestnut coloured hair, the bloody roots still clinging to the back of the note. Oh God. A flash of her face as the hair had been ripped from her head formed in my mind. The bastard!

My stomach rolled as a flash of the man who had left this note, filled my head. The cold rage that emanated from him, made a shiver go up my spine. He was capable of any atrocity in his quest. It was an obsession that consumed him.

I held the letter and looked down to read the spidery swirl of his handwriting.

Dear Keira,
You failed this test. I've been watching you since before you left California with Sean Jones. You thought that you could trick me, showing up early? You thought I'd just release your friend so easily? You underestimate my power. Or my goals. Don't try that again or next time it won't just be your friend's hair you'll find, it will be her HEAD!
Ditch the brother and pilot.
As they say on television, stay tuned for the next episode!
DH

Sean held the lock of hair in his fingers as he stood beside me, reading the note. "The slimy coward! He's playing us. He hurt Gwen!" I could hear his teeth grind together.

I folded the note and slipped it into my pocket, next to the black stone. "He knew all about us. He's been watching our every move right from the jump." My mind was going a mile a minute, right past the old guy with the big moustache that kept trying to hitch-hike onto my thoughts.

If Gwen had really escaped, why hadn't we heard that from the police? That would be the logical place she'd turn to once she was free. But for all I knew, he might have even got to the police. If she'd got away, perhaps they'd turn her over to him again.

Right now, the only people I could trust were Sean and Roy. Alistair might even be in David Holmes's employ. Even though I hadn't picked up any vibes from him about that, I couldn't take a chance.

I left Sean and wandered out of the room, checking for any clues or impressions that might have been left. Outside the tiny bathroom that was set under a stairwell, my hands roamed over the wooden frame. A picture of a mountain of a man, holding his stomach in pain flared before going black. And Gwen, she'd been in this room. She had something to do with the big guy's pain.

"You go girl," I said aloud.

I called to Sean to join me when I went back into the room where she'd been held. Sean joined me at the blood spot next to the pillow. His eyes met mine. "I know what you want. I agree. It's worth a shot."

We joined hands and with my other hand, I touched the bloody print.

The jolt of power was there immediately. Gwen. I pictured her in my mind, laying there. It was clear as a bell, the pain and fear she'd felt, but there was nothing, no clue as to where she was now.

This confirmed my worst fears. If this David Holmes had recaptured Gwen, he was using his power to shield her from me—creating some kind of impenetrable wall around her that my mind couldn't break.

Sean nodded as he spoke. "She's not free. He still has her."

TWENTY EIGHT

The frustration and defeat weighed on Sean. He slumped in the passenger seat when we drove away from the house. Even the anger that he normally lashed out on me had abandoned him when he looked down at the floor of the Audi.

"You know, Gwen is the kindest, most gentle person I've ever known." He sighed. "When she was still in high school she had a girlfriend, Esther, whose brother was in a motorcycle accident. She stayed with Esther all night in the hospital while they waited for the surgery to finish. Even though, Gwen had finals to write the next day, she refused to leave Esther. It meant she might not have gotten high enough grades to get accepted into university, but she didn't care."

I thought of Gwen and me together, facing that demon in my grandmother's room. Most people would have run out of the house screaming but she'd stayed to help me, risking her own safety. "Yeah, she's special all right," I said. I took a deep breath and looked over at him. "I really wish it was me instead of her that Holmes had taken."

He nodded. "I believe you." He glanced behind him and then looked over at me. "Roy and Alistair are right behind us." He looked at me again, "We really don't know where we go from here to find her."

"I know. And the note...he wants me alone, Sean." I looked over at him.

He shook his head. "That isn't going to happen. For all we know Gwen might already be dead. And if she isn't, I don't think he's going to let her escape." His brow furrowed. "He's been calling all the shots. We need to get a step ahead of him."

"But how? I got an impression of him, from handling the note, but no indication of where he is. He could be anywhere. He's been tracking us since California, and probably before that even. I really think he needs to know that I'm alone before he'll let me know his next move. It's the only thing we can do." My palms were sweaty on the steering wheel. Much as the thought of facing him alone scared the hell out of me, it was the only way that I could see getting us anywhere. I refused to believe that Gwen was dead.

"I don't like it. I agree we can let Alistair go back to his job, take him out of the equation...maybe even Roy as well. But I doubt he's going to do it." He looked straight ahead, his brow furrowed. He no longer bothered trying to block his thoughts from me, which was a good sign. There was no way he was going to be waved off in his attempt to find Gwen but he wasn't above making it look like he had.

"I don't think that Alistair is part of Holmes' crew but just in case, we need to give him the impression that we've gone our separate ways. I'll call Roy and bring him up to speed with that. It may look like Roy and I aren't with you anymore, but we'll be close by, in constant contact." He reached over and his fingers gripped my arm, "You don't go anywhere without letting me know first. Understand?"

I nodded even though I wasn't sure I would do that. Part of me desperately wanted Sean and Roy with me when I confronted Holmes but from the sinking feeling in my gut, I knew it had to be just me, going it alone.

***

I checked in once more at the hotel in Bantry where we stayed the night before. This time, I needed to make a show of the fact that I was there by myself. Even though my bones ached from the stress and sleeplessness, I forced myself to go to the little shop in the hotel to buy some clothes. The little cotton dress I'd put on in California at Jody's house was starting to feel really old. I sighed. Jody's house seemed like eons ago. The dress was dirty and I needed something more practical.

A half hour later, with new yoga pants, sweatshirts and underwear, I stopped at the front desk to inquire about dinner, and make a reservation for one. I kept looking over my shoulder, expecting someone who might be a Holmes operative to be lurking behind a potted plant. But aside from a family browsing through touristy brochures, the foyer was empty.

I glanced at my cell phone as I walked down the hallway to catch the elevator to my room. There was nothing. Not even a text from Holmes. He was playing a game of cat and mouse with me and it was getting me more and more cheesed off. Patience had never been my strong suit. Even Sean hadn't left a text to let me know where he and Roy were.

There was nothing I could do but wait. In the meantime, I poured a bath and soaked in the hot perfumed water for almost an hour, the cell phone within arm's reach on the floor. When I got out and got dressed it finally beeped with a message.

I grabbed it from the dresser and peered at it. My gut did a flip flop as I saw it was from an Unknown name and number. Holmes. It had to be.

I clicked the message icon and read,

> You will receive instructions later. No tricks this
> time or else. Your grandfather, David.

Even though my hands were itching to blast back a message asking about Gwen, I made myself pause for a moment. He had made it a point to sign 'grandfather'. The blood connection must mean more to him than it certainly did to me. Maybe there was a way of capitalizing on that.

Plus, it was obvious that he felt that he was in total control (which I had to admit, it looked like) but I needed to shake him up a bit, without risking Gwen.

I took a deep breath and carefully composed my answer.

> Grandfather, I need to see proof that you still have
> Gwen and that she is alive. If I don't hear from
> you, I'm leaving for Canada tomorrow.
> Your granddaughter,
> Keira

I almost gagged writing the grandfather and granddaughter stuff, but whatever worked, right?

After slipping the phone into my bag, I walked out of the room to go down to dinner, even though food was the last thing on my mind. But, if we were playing a game and he had someone watching me, I needed to show more confidence and control than I'd any right to claim.

I'd barely had a sip of the vodka gimlet, sitting at the table overlooking the ocean when my phone buzzed. Again, with a steady nonchalance, I lifted it from my bag and read,

> Keira, if you are as good as you think you are,
> you'll know the answer to your question about
> Gwen. Enjoy your dinner and get a good night's
> sleep. You're leaving tomorrow...but not for
> Canada

I glanced around at the dining room, suddenly feeling eyes

on me. The dining room was only half full and mostly with families or couples. I pushed the drink away and took long measured breaths, lowering my barriers to other people's thoughts.

The table next to me where an elderly couple and their daughter sat, was totally innocent, thinking of the day they'd spent sightseeing some old castle. Again, the next table with the young family revealed snippets centered on the new addition, the woman pregnant.

Again and again, I invaded the heads of the other diners but there was nothing out of the ordinary. Certainly no dark secrets of working for the lunatic who was my grandfather.

And what about Gwen? Did he even have her? He made it sound like I should be able to intuit how she was and even where. But there had been a barrier he'd put around her. Maybe, he was going to let that wall down.

When my dinner arrived, I ate as fast as I could. I didn't have much of an appetite, but I had hardly eaten anything all day and I needed the energy. I got out of my seat and signed for the bill when the waiter appeared.

The elevator took forever, going up to the top floor. There was only one way to channel into Gwen's whereabouts and I needed to focus all my energy in the quiet of my room.

Entering the room, my mouth fell open and I stared. Sean sat in the upholstered chair, gazing out at the ocean.

TWENTY NINE

H ow did you get in?" I set the bag down and walked over to where he sat. "Did anyone see you?"

"No. I made sure of that. Roy's next door. He booked a room for us but I didn't feel right leaving you on your own." He stood up and his face was flinty looking down at me. "Plus, I know you intended to take off on your own. I'm not letting you out of my sight until I find my sister."

"Sean...I didn't mean to lie to you but I *had* to. You shouldn't be here. I thought you were going to stay away until I called." Shit! Someone might have seen him despite what he thought. He might have just foiled the whole thing.

"Trust me, Keira, I didn't 'foil' anything!"

My jaw almost fell off my face. He'd read my mind, just like Nana had always done. It gave me an idea.

"I heard from Holmes. He's got people watching me, even here at the hotel. But he told me that I should be able to connect with Gwen telepathically. I haven't yet, and now that you're here, we might as well give it a go." I sat down on the bed and patted the spot next to me.

His head jerked back but then he sighed. "When were you going to tell me he contacted you? Or were you going to tell me at all?"

I rubbed the heels of my hands into my eyes. Actually, I wasn't going to tell him but now he knew. "Just get over here and hold my hand, will you? I've got a feeling that something's changed. We'll be able to reach her."

He sat down beside me. His hand fumbled as his fingers laced through mine. Again, the feeling of power and clarity surged in my body from his touch. If he wasn't the most arrogant, insufferable guy I'd ever met, it might be a blast to have....

NO! It came loud and clear, blaring from his mind.

My cheeks became red hot flares. Hell, I was tired as the walking dead and I'd let my mind wander. So sue me! It had been a day...No, make that *three* days, going on no sleep and little food!

He edged to the side so that only our hands touched. He underlined his mental message with body language.

"Okay, Gwen." My eyes closed and I took a few deep breaths, focusing all my energy on my friend. I saw her. She was sitting in what looked like an airline or bus seat. Her eyes opened wide and I could hear her silent cry, '*Keira*?'. And then Sean's name. Oh my God! She knew we were both there!

"*Where are you Gwen? Are you alright?*" Would she be able to catch my question? Please, please, please let it work!

Finally, the thought drifted into my mind, barely there, but there nonetheless.

"*Jody. She knows you, Keira.*"

I felt Sean's head turn to face me. The look in his eyes showed puzzlement mixed with relief. But none of this made sense. How was Jody involved when she was in Malaysia? And why was Gwen with her?

"*Are you safe, Gwen? Where exactly are you?*"

The sensation of numbing pain from her wrists and ankles, a red throbbing flash emanating from Gwen told me she was still captive. How could she be captive if she was with Jody?

Oh no. Jody and Holmes were working together. That's why I hadn't been able to connect with Gwen after her escape. Jody had been blocking me. But now Holmes ordered her to lift the block.

"*...a plane. It's not a big one, so we're not going far.*"

And then the wall was back. I could almost feel it slam shut like a steel door.

I turned to Sean and felt tears sting the back of my eyes. Relief that she was alive fought with frustration that Holmes still had her. "Did you catch all that?" The heavy sigh that rushed from his chest told me he had.

"Now we wait." His hand lifted to cup his forehead, "Shit!"

"You've got to leave. Holmes has people watching. If he knows you and Roy are still around, who knows what he'll do?" I propped myself up on my elbow and scowled at him.

"How many times do I have to tell you, no one could see me?" He sat up and squeezed my hand for good measure.

"What? Like now you're going to tell me you were invisible? Shit Sean! This is Gwen's life you're risking!" I got up and walked to the door.

As I was about to open it, his hand covered mine. "Stop!" He looked down at the floor for a few moments, thinking hard like he was trying to come to some decision. But the bastard was guarding his thoughts as well as Jody ever had.

His face was haggard and eyes bloodshot when he looked at me. "I'm not who you think I am."

THIRTY

My shoulders slumped as I let out a sigh. Not something else, please Lord. How much more could I take of this nightmare? "Who are you then, if not Gwen's brother? You're not with Holmes, so I give up." I stormed over to the bed and pulled the pillow over my head. No more!

I felt his fingers tugging the pillow away, and his face hovered above me. He slumped down onto the bed and his gaze held me captive with its intensity.

"I have the same kind of powers your grandmother had. We met only once and I knew I had to get away from her. I don't like being involved in any of this. She tried to recruit me but I turned her down. It's why I took a job so far from Kingston. "

"But why?" I pulled myself up to sit beside him. It was incredible. I'd gone to California to meet with Jody to learn more about the nature of the gifts I had. And all this time *Sean* had this power?

"I just want to live a normal life, that's why. I know about The Veil.

"Really."

"Yes, *really*. And furthermore, I am very familiar with how bad things can get when you tamper with the supernatural. The fact that we're in this mess with Gwen proves it. Your grandfather is not just crazy, Keira. He's possessed. You know that, right?" His fingers curled around mine, but this time the energy was more controlled. Instead of a jolting sensation, it was more of a low hum.

"You mean demonic possession, don't you?"I took a deep breath and let it out slowly as I nodded. "Yeah, I think you're right. I picked up on a really strange vibe when I touched his letter."

"Strange? What do you mean?"

I closed my eyes recalling the sensation. "It's hard to put into words. It was rage, but almost for anger's sake. But I took it to mean that he's more obsessed than anything else." I tilted my head at Sean. "But 'obsessed' is the wrong word, isn't it?" I hardly dared to say it but it was out there now. "Possessed is the right one."

He nodded. "It's not like the Exorcist but it's there. When he first started dabbling in this, his character weaknesses left him vulnerable to possession. He doesn't even know it, why he wants and does the things he does. But that's part of the insidious power of evil. He thinks he's in the driver's seat but he isn't."

"And that's why you didn't want Gwen involved with me. You were afraid something like this could happen to her."

"Your grandmother didn't tell you everything. She warned you...but she wasn't entirely forthcoming about the risks."

I scoffed. "I saw enough of the dangers, believe me."

"No, you didn't. She never warned you about getting beguiled, did she?"

"Beguiled?"

He nodded. "Yeah. When you expose yourself to the afterlife, you become vulnerable to the dark forces that exist there. They're sly and tricksey. You become deluded over time. The more exposure, like radiation—the more it can weaken you. Your grandfather is proof of that."

I wasn't buying it. "But my grandmother, she was involved in working with spirits most of her life, yet she remained true to herself and ultimately goodness. I don't see how you can just turn your back on what is essentially part of who you are."

He snorted, "Well I'm not turning my back now, am I?" He looked over at me and his jaw muscle twitched. "When this is over and we have my sister back, I will do everything I can to persuade her to leave this stuff alone. You should too."

It was the old Sean back again scowling at me. There was no way we'd ever agree. I have to admit that knowing he had been recruited by Nana before I'd shown up stung. I'd had enough of dealing with Sean for one night. "I'm going to bed. I'll check the hallway and if it's clear, you go back to your room."

"Nope." He swung around and tucked the pillow under his head. "It's not just that I don't trust you to up and leave Roy and I when you hear from Holmes. Seeing as how I'm into this up to my ears, it's better for both of us to stick together. I'm your Guardian for this next part."

I glared at him and thrust my hand in my pocket, holding the black tourmaline stone out. "I have this for protection. You need to leave." The nerve of the guy! He may be *almost* my equal (I still didn't believe he could do the things I could!) and he was bossing me around! I was too tired for his BS any longer.

"If you're worried that I'll make a pass...don't. That's not why I want to stay and besides...I think I have more to worry about in that respect from you, judging by your thoughts earlier." If he didn't smile, totally disarming me with the dimple, I would have belted him.

"Love yourself, much?" I smiled and then went into the bathroom to change into my night shirt and get ready for bed.

Ten minutes later, his soft snores made me sigh. How was I ever going to be able to sleep with that racket?

THIRTY ONE

When I woke up, Sean was gone. My heart sank. I'll admit it, okay? I still didn't like the way he'd pushed himself into my room and refused to leave; the guy has serious control issues. And yet… I had to admit that I'd slept better than I had in a long time. A very long time. I couldn't remember the last time I awoke feeling so rested.

Dammit!

And now he was gone.

I popped out of bed and grabbed my cell phone. It was seven in the morning. I slept for twelve hours! My eyes narrowed. There was still no message from Holmes, even though he'd said he would contact me. It would be more of the waiting game that I detested.

I was tempted to text Sean to see what he was up to but chose to make coffee instead. The less contact with him, especially with Holmes having me watched, the better. When I came out of the shower, ten minutes later, I sat in the chair by the window, sipping coffee and watching the sea gulls swoop above the rocky shoreline.

At the beep of my cell phone, my heart leapt into my throat. I grabbed it from the table and read,

This is your last warning. Ditch the brother and go to the airport alone. There's a plane leaving at twelve twenty for Southhampton. I'll be in touch when you arrive there. Your Grandfather

He knew that Sean was still with me! Dammit! I'd told him that someone probably saw him coming into my room. He had to get it through his thick skull that he was endangering Gwen!

Gwen...she responded when I reached out to her last night. She even knew Sean was with me. My hand rose to thunk into my forehead. Of course! Jody had been with her! Jody had lifted the wall and then slammed it shut again! Jody had picked up on Sean's presence somehow. How stupid of us to overlook that and not give Gwen a warning.

Still, I couldn't discount the possibility that Sean had been seen by one of Holmes's minions. I had to do this alone. I rose from the chair. Even though it was still too early to go to the airport for the flight, I had to get out of there before Sean showed up again. He'd know with a glance that Holmes had contacted me.

I threw my things in the small carry-on bag and looked both ways down the hall before venturing out. Darting past the elevator, I raced to the stairwell. There was no way I could take a chance of running into Roy or Sean...especially Sean. I made my way to the foyer and out the door.

The Audi was parked at the far end of the lot and as I raced to it, I passed Roy's rental car. Good. At least I knew they were still there and wouldn't spot me somewhere on the road going back through the small town.

I threw my bag into the passenger seat and got behind the wheel. When I turned the key in the ignition, there was only a clicking sound. "Come on!" I tried it again and the clicks became softer, like the battery was dying. "Shit!" I pounded the palms of my hands against the steering wheel.

At the tap on the glass next to my shoulder, I spun around.

"Going somewhere?" Sean's eyes were narrow. Behind him, Roy stood with his hands thrust deep in his pockets, glaring at me.

My hands gripped the door handle and I threw it wide. "What did you do to this car? I was going into town for...for aspirin and you wrecked the engine? Thanks!"

He leaned past my shoulder looking at the seat beside me. "Looks like you weren't coming back though. Why else would you bring your luggage? You heard from him, didn't you?"

Roy stepped forward. "Look Keira, we need each other right now. I was kidnapped by these goons. You can't go alone."

"I don't agree, Roy. He wants me. If I go ALONE, Gwen has a chance of getting out of this. Especially if I can convince Holmes that I'll do whatever it is he wants of me." I turned to Sean, "Fix this car. You broke it, I know you did!"

Sean speared me with his eyes, trying to read my thoughts. But I was a step ahead of him there.   "What did he say, Keira? Where were you off to?"

"It was Jody, Sean. She felt your presence when we made contact with Gwen last night. Don't you see? We have to play this HIS way or Gwen is done for." My shoulders slumped and I looked down at the useless steering wheel. "Just go away and let me handle this." I wasn't looking forward to it, but it was something I had to do—alone. Now to guard my thoughts from Sean.

His arm shot forward, pushing me back in the seat while his hand rummaged in my bag. He scooped the cell phone out and then stepped back, pushing the button to read the message from Holmes. Roy hunched forward peering past Sean's arm.

He spun around to face me. "Southampton? You were flying to England, on a commercial flight?" He gripped Sean's arm. "We'll catch another flight and get there before Keira does." He turned to me again, "When you land, we'll be there." He looked over to Sean. "Along with the police."

Sean tugged his arm away, "No. No police. She's right about that much, Roy. But we'll be there, following at a safe distance." He was already on his way to the front of the car. "Lift the hood."

A plan was starting to formulate in my mind and I needed to be really careful with my thoughts. I flipped the lever of the hood and sat waiting. I'd need to contact Holmes and change the plane and destination. It might slow me down but at least I'd be able to get away from Roy and Sean. Whatever plan they were cooking up had too many chances of failing.

And Gwen would pay the price.

THIRTY TWO

I sat in the dining room of the hotel, trying to swallow the breakfast I'd ordered. Sean and Roy were already on their way to catch a different flight than the one Holmes instructed me to take and I was to give them an hour's head start before driving to the airport. Someone might have seen the three of us together in the parking lot but at least we were separated now.

The cell phone on my lap vibrated and I picked it up. It was just Roy telling me he'd made a connection and that they'd be in Southampton at one. Well, they'd be there without me, if my luck held.

I opened the message from Holmes and typed a reply.

> We need to change flights. I'll go to England but
> not to Southampton. You want me to come alone?
> That's the only way I can guarantee it

I clicked the send button and then my eyes closed, saying a

silent prayer. Hopefully, he would know that it wasn't a trick of some sort.

Immediately the cell phone buzzed again.

Fine. Catch the next flight at two to Bournemouth.
Finally, you are acting in your own best interest.
There's hope for you yet.
I'll be in touch

'My own best interest'? I was only doing this for Gwen. What the hell did he want from me? The first message, the one he'd given Roy stated that he wanted me to stop meddling. And by that, I knew it was to stop doing any kind of work with anything supernatural. But the niggling of dread in my chest was telling me he wanted more from me.

And what was Jody getting out of all this? It was then that I remembered that I hadn't spoken to my parents since this nightmare started. I might never get the chance again if my plans went south. I pushed the plate of eggs aside and hit the button to dial my parents.

When Mom answered, my eyes welled with tears and it was hard to speak past the lump in my throat.

"Keira? Are you there?"

"Hi Mom. How are you doing?"

"Is everything alright? Why are you calling at this hour? Thank goodness I'm the early riser in this family!"

"What are you talking about? It's 11:00 in the morning."

She laughed. "Silly! It's six am here!"

"Oh. Yeah. Right. Sorry, my bad. I just wanted to check in with you guys is all." Just hearing her voice, bright eyed and bushy tailed was a knife in my heart, but I wanted—no, needed to hear her voice one last time. "So… what's going on? Got any big plans for Easter?" I hunched over the table, hiding my face with my hand on my forehead. All the while, she told me about her plans for Easter and what she and Dad were doing for the next little while, tears filled my eyes. Would I even be alive to join them for Easter? Her question about my LA visit with Jody, brought me out of my funk. I took a deep breath.

"You were right about Jody, Mom. She is a nasty piece of work."

The connection broke up for a second and then she asked the question I was dreading. "Where are you? Is Gwen with you?"

"I'm in Ireland, near Cork. Gwen's not here right now. I'm supposed to meet up with her in England later today."

She must have sensed the tension in my voice because her next question was "What's wrong, Keira? Are you all right?"

For just a moment I was tempted to break down in tears and spill my problems onto her shoulders, just like I'd done when I was younger, but instead I forced a cheeriness in my voice. There was no need to get her frantic with worry. What good would it do? It sure wouldn't fix the problem I was facing.

"I'm fine Mom. I just wanted to hear your voice and say I love you."

"Now you're *really* scaring me." Her light laugh followed and I couldn't help smiling.

"What? I can't call you and tell you that? I don't do it enough. Can you put Daddy on the phone?" I needed to hear his voice too. If I was being maudlin, I might as well go all in.

She laughed again. "He's still asleep. It's only six o'clock in the morning here, you know! I'll have him call you when he gets up."

"Okay, Mom. I'll talk to you later." I clicked off the phone and sat still for a few minutes, picturing the two of them, starting their day.

For the first time, I wished I'd never gone to Kingston and met my grandmother. But there was no sense thinking this way. I was in it, as Sean had said, 'up to my ears.'

It was time to leave for the airport.

THIRTY THREE

It was almost five by the time I cleared customs and entered the main area of the Bournemouth airport. People hustled to and fro, excited about meeting relatives or embarking on their trip. I bought a coffee and then took a seat near the main entry, waiting once more for the next instruction.

I didn't have long to wait. The phone buzzed and I slid it from my purse.

> You are to come to Priory Bay, on the Isle of Wight. Follow the signs to The Priory Bay Estate. Ensure you bring the protective stone that your grandmother gave you. The Isle is home to many spirits. Most assuredly they will recognize you, and I can't guarantee that you won't be attacked as you travel. I expect you no later than nine PM. Arrive after that time and your friend will become one of the Isle's afterlife

I looked all around me. Someone *was* watching me, but once again I saw nothing, and sensed nothing.

That bastard! I slipped the phone into my purse and hurried to one of the car rental places. I had only four hours to get to a place, an *island* at that! Thank God for the GPS app on my phone.

***

Despite my GPS app, there were a few wrong turns. Even so, I managed a late booking on the ferry to the island. Why did Holmes have to make this such a road rally to find him? My fingers tapped nervously on the steering wheel as I waited in the lineup of cars and trucks waiting to board. I glanced at the clock on the dashboard. It was still early, just a little after six but even so, there was no way I'd chance being late.

After parking the car, I climbed the stairs to go to the upper decks. I grabbed a coffee from a small shop and then found a seat off to one side, away from the cheerful noise of young families. My hand slipped into the pocket of my jeans, once more checking that the black stone was there. He'd told me to bring it but I would have anyways. Nana had given me that stone for protection from evil spirits and besides that, it was like a piece of her with me all the time.

I finished my coffee and then closed my eyes, leaning back in the seat. If only she were with me now, about to face Holmes. Whether it was the calm before the storm, a chance to catch my breath, or the small vibration of the ship's engines, I felt myself become lulled into a sense of calm. The sounds around me all faded and there was only me, my mind clear of everything around me.

In my mind's eye, a blurred grey shape began to take form, coming closer from a sea of mist. It was a woman, an old woman, moving towards me, her hand extended before her. I knew it was her. Nana. Her form took shape and I heard her whisper my name. Her eyes were that same deep blue I saw every day in the mirror, and her hair was loosely piled on her head.

'Nana, please help me.' I could feel my chin quiver and my throat grow tight, the tears threatening to burst forth.

'Keira, remember what I told you about fear. Use it, don't be over-powered by it. You are stronger than you know.' Her words tore at my heart. She's said those same words when she was alive and I'd give anything for her to be with me when I faced the evil that my grandfather was.

But she wasn't. Gradually the impression of her in my mind faded. I was alone in this. She had believed in me, so why couldn't I? I took slow measured breaths until the P.A. system broke through my thoughts, announcing our arrival in Yarmouth. The forty minutes had gone by in the blink of an eye and I was starting the final leg of my journey.

I opened my eyes and gave my head a small shake to clear it. I had to get below decks to my car. As I was about to get up, I looked at the empty seat next to me and gasped. A red rose sat there! Nana's favourite flower. I scooped it up and sniffed the sweet scent, the aroma filling me.

"Let's do this," I said aloud.

When I made my way back to the small rental car, I set the cell phone on the dash and clicked it on, resuming the directions for getting to this Priory Bay and the Estate my grandfather owned.

As soon as the car came off the ferry, an oppressive wave washed over me so strongly my head pressed back into the headrest. The air was like lead; heavier and hard to breathe. The ancient force of the multitude of ley lines crossing the island was a potent force. Even the historic stone and clapboard homes I passed were smudged with a film of evil. I turned the car's heat up a notch when the skin on my arms puckered into tingling bumps. It was no wonder Holmes had been drawn to this place—the most haunted island in the world.

My eyes opened wide when I passed a cemetery and saw shadowy forms hovering between the stones. My hand dropped from the steering wheel and my fingers rested on the stone in my pocket, the only thing protecting me right then.

But even that didn't stop the young girl at the side of the road from stepping in the path before me. She appeared so... *real*; except she cast no shadow. Her spectral gaze and the period clothes confirmed that she was a spirit. I drove right through her, feeling icy air on me as I passed through her presence.

I glanced in the rear view mirror at the car a few hundred feet behind me. The driver hadn't seen what I'd seen or he would surely have braked. But it continued at the same speed.

The voice of the navigation app chirped at me; I saw up ahead the turn that it indicated was coming up. There was only fifteen minutes until I would meet my grandfather.

THIRTY FOUR

Gwen

She woke up with a start, her gaze flitting about the room. It was a different location, *again*! This room was bright with large, multi paned windows overlooking a garden and pool. In the distance the blue of the ocean peeked through the many trees bordering the lawn.

They'd left her alone in what looked like some kind of living room or parlour, furnished with gold upholstered sofas and chairs centered on an oriental rug. It didn't matter. Her hands and feet were bound tight to the heavy wooden chair. But it was a welcome break from that horrible Jody woman and Keith. Holmes never bothered with her anymore. Whatever information he wanted, he'd given up on getting it from her.

From the cast of the light shining in through the windows, she'd guess it was about three in the afternoon. The hunger pangs had given way to a weary weakness. The drugs they kept shooting into her arm were causing swells of dizziness and nausea as she sat there.

The only glimmer of hope, when she'd sensed Sean and Keira the night before, was snuffed short when Jody stepped into the room. At a signal from Holmes the communication had vanished and she was left feeling the lowest point yet in this horrible nightmare.

The heavy and ornate wooden door at the opposite end of the room opened wide and Jody strode in. She'd changed out of the ivory pantsuit and now sported her true colour—black slacks and a turtle neck. From her hand a bulging department store bag swung high.

"It's time to clean you up. David is expecting Keira and it wouldn't do to let her see you like this. I got you a fresh set of clothes." She smiled but the smile didn't extend to her eyes.

She didn't mention Sean! Did that mean they'd done something to him? Keira and Sean had been together, the only hope that she had of somehow getting away from these crazies.

"Your brother is fine. But Keira gave him the slip. Lucky for you, I'd say."

Shit! She had to try to guard her thoughts from the horrid woman. She was actually as good as Keira had been at reading her mind.

"Better. Much better than Keira." There was an wicked glint in Jody's dark eyes.

Keith stepped into the room, holding a hypodermic needle in his hand. Oh God! Not another needle. Gwen tugged at the restraints holding her arms, but it was no use. The straps bit into her flesh all the harder.

"Only give her half the dose. We want her subdued, not comatose." Jody spoke to Keith as he approached. "Then untie her. She's going upstairs to the bath."

Keith jabbed the needle into Gwen's upper arm and his gaze flickered to meet hers. "No tricks this time, girly. It isn't Joe you're dealing with now. I'll shoot you as quick as look at you." The softness of his voice made her skin crawl. There was no doubt he meant every word.

She glanced down at the syringe and the network of blue

bruises on her arm. This had to be like the tenth needle she'd been shot with. Her muscles ached as the liquid spread through the tissue. "You can't shoot me. Your boss needs me alive to get Keira here."

"She's already on her way. And Holmes might want you alive, but..." He pulled the needle out. "...shit happens sometimes. Take my advice and save yourself the trouble." He set the needle on a side table and then Gwen felt his fingers working at the strap on her ankle.

She stretched her leg out, and the pain of the sudden circulation of blood there made her wince. Soon the drug they'd given her would start to numb her mind, a mixed blessing.

Keith's fingers dug into the muscle of her upper arm, tugging her to her feet. "Let's go."

Any thoughts of attempting an escape were lost in the fog that mushroomed in her brain. Her feet were blocks of wood, stumbling across the room and a couple of times she felt dizzy to the point that she stumbled. Keith might not be as tall as she was but he was strong as a bear, keeping her upright and then yanking her up the set of stairs.

When they came to the bathroom, Keith shoved her inside while Jody followed. Gwen looked around the small but elegantly laid out bathroom, the antique claw footed bath filled with water and the ornate vanity with the marble top.

"Here." Jody set the bag of clothes on the counter. "Keith will be just outside. I'll leave you to it." For the first time, there was unease in Jody's eyes before she hurried out the door.

When it closed behind her, Gwen gripped the side of the vanity, steadying herself while gazing at her reflection in the mirror. She looked haggard with dark circles under her eyes and skin the colour of death. Her hair hung in limp strings over the shoulders of her shirt, stained with droplets of blood. Her hand rose and felt the sore spot where a handful of hair had been ripped out. There was a crusty ridge of blood dried to the ragged patch of her scalp.

Her breath froze in her throat when the hazy face appeared

in the mirror. It was a woman standing behind her, next to the tub of water. Even through the thin mist on the mirror, the woman's eyes and mouth showed sympathy. Gwen spun around, unsure if her eyes were playing tricks on her, that this apparition was actually there.

"Gwen."

The woman's mouth hadn't moved and the word was more in Gwen's head than in the small room. Her heart was beating fast but she managed to whisper as she stared at the ghost. "Who are you?"

"It doesn't matter. I'm here to help. I don't have long so listen carefully if you want to live."

At that point Gwen was ready to anything to escape this nightmare and help Keira and Sean. There was no doubt in her mind that Holmes was an evil man who wouldn't let her live to tell the tale. As for Keira...she didn't know what Keira would do once she arrived.

THIRTY FIVE

I glanced up at the leering gargoyles perched on each of the two stone pillars as I wheeled the car onto the estate. The last of the sun's rays cast shadows from the looming trees lining the drive. If the rest of the island along the way had been eerie, it had nothing on this place. The drive over was through an atmosphere of oppressive sadness and woe. This estate exuded evil. A knot of dread seized my gut and my palms were slippery on the steering wheel.

When I wheeled around a sharp bend in the long driveway, the stone, three story house was about fifty feet away. There was only one black Suburban SUV parked out front but at the rear of the property an orange helicopter sat like a giant bug. I parked the car a little ways from the building and leaned over the steering wheel, taking in the acres of lawn and forest extending into the distance. It was totally secluded—the perfect place for whatever nastiness Holmes had planned.

I took a deep breath and got out of the car. As I walked to the ivy covered portico, the front door opened and a portly, old man in a sports jacket and dark trousers stepped out. His eyes pierced me and then a slow smile spread below the ivory moustache.

"Keira. We meet at last. I'm your grandfather." His hands clasped behind his back and his chest and round stomach bulged above his pants. There was a murky green aura that emanated from his head becoming grey as it descended over his body.

If I hadn't known it before, it was plain as anything to me now that he was downright possessed. There was no way I was getting anywhere close to him. I stopped and crossed my arms over my chest, "Where's Gwen?"

"She's sitting down to dinner as we speak. Come in. You're right on time." He turned slightly and beckoned to me like we were old friends meeting for a drink, sharing gossip. Another man now filled the doorway behind him, holding a gun pointed to the sky, in front of his shoulder.

The threat was clear. But something told me that Holmes hadn't asked me here to kill me. He had plenty of opportunities to do that before. "I'm not going anywhere until I see Gwen. Get her."

We stared at each other for a few beats before Holmes nodded to the other guy and then turned to me. "It doesn't have to be like this you know. We could work together. There's no limit to what we can accomplish. Immortality even. Wouldn't you like to have known Pamela longer? She too, was stubborn, persisting in her silly work."

"Don't you *dare* to say her name! As far as I'm concerned you were just a sperm donor. You're no grandfather or anything to me or her." I clenched my fists, only realizing then that I had taken a step towards him. In addition to being possessed, he was totally batshit crazy. I wanted nothing more than to knock him aside and run in the house to get Gwen. But I was outnumbered and his hired hand had a gun.

My eyes opened wide when Gwen appeared in the doorway, the thug's hand gripping her arm. Even from where I stood, I could see the vacant glaze of her eyes, blinking slowly. They'd drugged her and now she was like a rag doll being propped up in a baggy blue dress.

"Gwen? Come over here." My heart wrenched as I saw my words drift past her. It didn't look like she even recognized me. Her body was there but her mind had been hollowed out. She would be no help in any plan to get her out of there.

At another nod from Holmes, Gwen was yanked back into the building. If I could only touch her and ignite some kernel of consciousness with the energy that had always sparked between us. It looked like I would have no choice but to go inside and see what Holmes expected of me.

I affected a casual voice and even managed a smile. "What's for dinner?" I stepped over and looked past Holmes into the house. Standing in the light of a chandelier that held millions of crystal tear drops, was Jody. She smirked when she saw me step by Holmes and enter the house. It just confirmed what I'd suspected— that she was working with him. But why?

She laughed and it was like a dagger to my gut. "You've still got some homework to do on masking your thoughts, Keira."

"And it looks like even with your *supposed* power, Jody, Holmes still wanted me. It must be tough being second fiddle all the time to Swanson women. But I suppose you should be used to it by now." I sneered at her, walking by, purposely jolting her with my shoulder. "My mother has so much more style and breeding than you. No wonder Dad threw you over."

Her hand shot out to fist in my hair and she jerked me towards her. Despite the stabbing pain, I couldn't resist. "Oh, so it was you who yanked Gwen's hair out. Typical skank move."

"Enough! Jody, let go of her hair." The icy command in Holmes's voice did the trick.

I rubbed at my scalp and then looked past the archway where a long table and sideboard told me that the dinner was being served in there. Gwen was probably there, barely able to sit upright on a chair.

"I don't know why you don't just kill her, David. She'll never work with you and I have more experience and power than she will ever have." Jody sniffed and held her chin high, glaring at me.

I turned to Holmes, "Yeah. Why not use her for whatever nasty scheme you have? You don't need me or Gwen. Just tell me what it is you want and I'm out of here. With Gwen, of course."

He crossed his arms over his chest and his eyes narrowed. "That's so like you isn't it, Keira? You flit from one thing to another. I know all about the courses in education...the social work, the photography and then getting kicked out of acting school. You couldn't finish anything if you tried. Even this dabbling in the paranormal scheme. It's just one more example of your usual pattern." He shook his head slowly. "A litany of failures."

Jody stepped closer to Holmes, "That's what I've been trying to tell you, David. She's useless to you."

"Be quiet, Jody! This is between my granddaughter and me. Go inside and check on Gwen." He shot a look at her that made her take a step back and then go off in a huff to the dining room.

But he wasn't through yet. He glared at me, "Your grandmother was just the start of your instruction in this sphere. It's time you assumed your true role, at my side to guide you."

The man was certifiable! What did he hope to accomplish? There was only one way to find out. "Okay. Say I agree? What is it you expect from me?"

"Keira, you will no longer work to transition spirits to a higher plane. That's got to stop, whether you agree to work by my side or not. Although, with your history, given time you'd probably lose interest in that anyway,. But I'm not getting younger and I can't wait for that to happen naturally."

My hands formed fists and I leaned closer to him. I had more than enough of being berated by the likes of him, a two bit hood. "It's not like that this time. This is what I was meant to do! Nana—"

"Pamela was a fool! I loved her once but she persisted in this crazy scheme when she could still be with me today. She should have *broken* The Veil, not protect it!" He shouted, while his face had gone an angry brick colour. With any luck he'd have a heart attack or stroke.

He waved trembling hands at me. "You know what will happen when The Veil ceases to exist? The laws that govern this world would no longer apply! Laws of physics, laws of time and space! I could be in two places at once! In any period of time, the future, past...anything! *Death itself* would no longer exist!" His face became calm and his gaze drifted to his own inner psychosis.

Watching him made my blood run cold. But it wasn't just him, it was the entity holding him in its grip. He was just a crazy old fool but the force that ruled him was powerful and would stop at nothing to achieve its goal. And that entity was shimmering inside his body. I could see it...feel the rage directed at me. My fingers slipped into my pocket and I grasped the black stone tight.

The slimey creature inside Holmes jerked back and Holmes stared at me. His eyes flashed red and then grew black as coal. "If you want your friend to live, you'll give up this so-called work you do. You'll work for me."

I had to buy time, convince him before he did something to Gwen. "Okay. But I need to know that Gwen is safe. Bring her out here again."

"I don't believe you, Keira. I too have talent in this game. You want to unite with her and over-power me. I know when you join hands, your energy is magnified. I'm not stupid." He stepped closer to me and his hand rose slowly to touch my arm.

I stumbled from the jolt of power that emanated from his fingers. My stomach rolled and I had to turn away and swallow the bile that rose in my throat. The energy was a black leech that drew from me. My legs tingled and then became numb. I fell back, barely catching myself with my hands before my head bounced off the floor.

He towered and swayed above me, reaching once more to touch me. I scrambled back, slipping on the polished marble surface. My chest heaved trying to catch my breath, and I peered around the room looking for something...some weapon to use against him. If he touched me once more, I would be lost. I knew it!

But there was nothing at hand and he kept advancing!

THIRTY SIX

Gwen...

It was all she could do to sit at the table, listening to the argument escalate to a shouting match in the foyer next to her. The spirit she'd encountered in the bathroom hadn't been wrong, when she warned that Keira would be defeated by the demon unless Gwen did as instructed. And from the sounds of it, the black energy that pulsed from Holmes extending to where she sat, she didn't have very much time.

Jody and Keith had bought into her numbed submission and now were in the arched opening, staring at the scene between Holmes and Keira. Gwen sneaked a glance around the room. Was the spirit here? She'd need her help to take out Jody and Keith before she could help Keira.

Whether it was the thought or just desperation in her trembling body, the woman's spirit once more appeared...and she wasn't alone! The form of a burly spectre and two children began to shimmer in the air at the other side of the room.

The male spirit nodded. A large cast iron warming tray that

was on the sideboard rose up above the table. As if it was shot from a catapult, it hurtled silently across the room, the edge of it slamming into the back of Keith's skull.

Jody swirled at the clang, to see Keith crumple to the floor. Before she could do anything, Gwen was out of the chair, racing at the woman. She hit her like a fullback football player, knocking her head and shoulders into the door frame. Gwen looked down at her and then the spirits descended on Jody, followed by every utensil and dish on the table smashing into her.

It had been enough to distract Holmes from advancing towards Keira. He glared at Gwen and turned his attention to her! Gwen's heart leapt into her throat at the red glimmer surrounding him. His hand rose and the veins in his neck popped high as he focused his murderous gaze on her. Whatever power he had, grasped at her, a steel vise closing on her chest.

She couldn't breathe and felt her ribcage begin bending! It had taken everything she had to leap out of the chair and tackle Jody! And now, tendrils of unseen steel were squeezing the life right out of her!

Gwen looked over at Keira, saw her scrambling to her feet and then raising her arm high. The black stone hit Holmes in the temple and bounced to the floor, dazing him. It was just for a split second, but the bands loosened enough that Gwen gasped, and lurched forward.

Holmes was once more straightening, a trickle of blood running down his cheek when the front door burst wide!

"SEAN!" What the hell was Sean doing there? It was the most welcome sight Gwen could ever imagine!

Sean took in the scene and bounded towards Holmes, landing a punch to his gut. His fists curled around Holmes's lapels and he hoisted him up, ramming him into the wall and pinning him there. He turned slightly and yelled, "Keira! Get Gwen!"

In a flash Keira was beside her, hugging her, the tears running down her face. "Are you okay? I thought they'd drugged you."

"They did! But the spirit—Alicia Adams— she helped me!" Gwen turned slightly looking down at the misty shapes who were beginning to fade. But they'd done their work! Jody's body was bloody and broken from all the objects hurled at her. Gwen smiled at the sight. That evil little woman had tricked her and done more to break her spirit than the other three ever could.

"Oh my God! I'm so sorry Gwen!" Keira once more pulled her into a fierce hug.

BANG!

At the deafening noise Keira jumped back! Keith had risen slightly, a trail of smoke lifting from the end of the gun barrel.

But it was Sean, the red hole in his back growing bigger by the minute, his body collapsing to the floor that made Gwen's heart stop.

THIRTY SEVEN

It all happened so fast! I was shoved to the floor when Keith ran past. He grabbed Holmes and dragged him through the foyer. "C'mon! We've got to get out of here!"

The old man was bleeding and dazed from the beating that Sean had laid on him. He stumbled, letting Keith pull him out the door.

Sean! I jumped beside Gwen kneeling next to Sean. His eyes were closed and his skin held a deathly pallor.

Gwen held his head in her lap. "Sean. No. Don't die." Her voice was a faint wail, almost coo'ing at him. But her fingers were frantic, pushing the lock of hair that had fallen to his forehead back. "No. No. You can't die, Sean!" Her tears fell onto his cheek.

His blood covered the floor around us. I peered at his chest. He wasn't breathing. Oh my God, it couldn't be true. "Sean?" Tears blinded me and my shoulders wracked with sobs. This couldn't be happening. "No, no, no! You can't die yet, Sean!"

At the tingling touch on my shoulder, I jerked around. It

was a spirit but not Sean's! Oh my God!

Nana! She smiled at me and then looked over to where Gwen was rocking back and forth, her voice a low keen in her throat.

"Remember your gift, Keira." The words sounded in my head and she faded from view. My chest leapt and I clutched Gwen's arm. It was still there, the energy thunderbolt surging between us!

"Gwen! We can save him! He's still here, don't you see? His spirit isn't hovering over us!" I slid my hand down and clutched hers in mine. "Hold his hand, Gwen! Sean is strong. As strong as you or me. He isn't meant to die yet."

Her eyes met mine. "Can we do this?" But she was already reaching for his hand, holding onto it for dear life.

The thread of hope was in her eyes as the three of us connected.

Just like on the ferry ride over, the world faded away. The whup-whup of the helicopter starting up, as its engines began to shriek and whine drifted away from the three of us.

Every atom in my body tingled with the current flowing through us. "*Sean. Sean Jones, come back to us. Your wound is healing.*" I closed my eyes and saw the wound, the bullet lodged between his ribs. It hadn't reached his heart! But the blood needed to stop seeping out of the wound. "*Close. Close and heal.*" I could feel it in my own back, the sharp pain of it. Breathing steadily, I willed it with every fibre of my being to heal. It lasted forever it seemed, the tears continuing to roll down my cheeks.

He coughed! And like that, the world resumed its shape and form; we were back in the stone building. Sean's eyes fluttered open and his voice was a whisper. "Gwen? You're safe."

I leaned over him and tears clouded my eyes! He was alive! We'd done it!

"Keira?" again the faint whisper.

"I'm calling for help." I hated to remove my hand from Gwen's and his, but my talent only went so far. I was no doctor and that was what he needed right then. But we'd done it!

"Don't speak, Sean. Just be still. You're going to be all right." Gwen's voice was soft and soothing in my ears as I pulled the phone out.

Oh my God. I peered at Gwen. "What's the number here? I don't think it's nine one, one...what is it?"

"Nine, nine, nine. I read it in a novel once. Try that." She leaned over and kissed Sean's forehead, holding him close again.

I had a hard time telling the emergency dispatch where I was. The words were hard to get past the lump in my throat as I sat watching Sean's chest rise and fall. I just knew he was going to make it and everything would be all right...for now at least.

David Holmes had escaped. Which reminded me...I got up and walked over to where Jody lay. She wasn't breathing and her eyes were open. But that witch would never see the light of day. She was an empty shell, the spark of her consciousness, her soul, gone on to the next realm. Thank God, I wouldn't have to ever deal with any part of her again. I would cry no tears for her.

Where her spirit had gone, no Veil was required.

THIRTY EIGHT

The next morning, my eyes creaked open, blinking a few times at the dull light sneaking into the hotel room from a grey sky. I rose from the bed, wondering if the past few days had only been a nightmare. I wish.

No it had been only too real. Sean was in the hospital after getting *shot*... and Gwen.

How could I look her in the eye after what she went through because of me? Who was I kidding, look me in the eye? It was more likely that she'd never want to lay eyes on me again.

My heart was heavy...I couldn't blame her in the slightest.

So that's that. I needed to get off this godforsaken island and put it all behind me. But first there were a couple of things to take care of.

I grabbed my laptop and cell phone and set them on the small table near the window. Flopping down in the chair, I punched the button to call Roy. He'd be with Gwen and I'd be able to talk to her.

He answered on the second ring. "Keira?"

"Hi Roy. Is Gwen with you? Can I talk to her?" My heart beat faster even though it was a heavy lump in my chest.

"Sure."

"Hi Keira." The usual bounce was missing from her voice.

"How is Sean?" I looked down, teasing a hangnail until it started to bleed. This was harder than I'd thought it would be and Gwen's voice was so cold.

"He's in recovery. The operation went well even though the doctors still can't figure why he didn't die."

I blew out a sigh of relief. "Thank God." My eyes welled with tears and I had to fight to control my voice. "Gwen, I'm really sorry about all this. I will make it up to you and Sean, I swear. I'm going home now." I inhaled. "Well, first I want to stop by my parents' house in New York. Let me know when you're back in Kingston. Please."

"I've got to go. I'm allowed in now to see my brother. Goodbye Keira."

Oh God. That goodbye sounded so *final*. I wiped the tears from my face and opened the laptop, sending an email to Mr. Thompson. Sean would never have to worry about money or keeping a job after the wire transfer.

Just one more call and then I'd get ready to leave.

"Keira? What's wrong?"

I forgot the time change. Again. Shit. "Mom?" The tears flowed freely now at the love and concern in my mother's voice. She must have known, because she sighed and told me to take my time. As if, I could help it.

After a few minutes, I took a deep breath, trying to shake it off enough to speak. "I'm still in the UK, Mom. But I'll be in New York later today. I need to see you and Daddy."

THIRTY NINE

Three weeks later...

It had been therapeutic spending time with my parents, getting my head around all that had happened. Mom and Dad were both horrified at Jody's role in all of it and felt responsible because they sent me out to see her in LA. Dad was overwhelmed with guilt for making the suggestion, and Mom felt just as badly for agreeing it was a good idea.

I didn't blame either of them; but more importantly, they didn't blame each other. When it comes to strong marriages, my parents set a high bar.

By the time I boarded my flight home (yes, I chartered a plane, but no, Roy was not at the controls) they had made it clear they wanted my career as a ghost whisperer to be over. Mom and Dad were all for me turning my back on the transitioning of spirits. The police still hadn't caught up with David Holmes, so that threat was very real. They were mainly worried about my well being

My well being? I was the only one who came through this

episode unscathed! Roy had been beaten, Gwen too, as well as pumped full of drugs; and Sean got shot! I came out of all of it without a scratch.

I wasn't ready to call it quits. I was almost there, sure; but despite all that happened, I knew this was what I was born to do.

But I couldn't do it alone.

Back in Kingston, I had one more thing to do. It was a visit that filled me with turmoil envisioning it, on the trip home from New York. But it was something that I had to do. Even Mom and Dad had agreed and they'd rather cut off their right arm than see me go through any more angst.

I wheeled the car into Gwen's house and my stomach became a hard knot of worry seeing Gwen's truck, and Sean's car parked out front. Well, it looked like everyone would be there. My feet were lead as I climbed the few steps and knocked on the door.

When it opened and Sean stood there, his blue denim shirt, highlighting the depth of colour in his eyes, my heart did a somersault before I squared my shoulders, meeting his icy glare. "Hi Sean. Can I come in?"

"Keira. I can't accept your money."

I'd heard it before. He'd emailed me at my parents, insisting I take it back. "Fine. Do whatever you want with it. Burn it, for all I care."

I brushed by him, making my way into the living room. But I paused in the archway, my gaze flitting from Devon, his ghostly wife hovering behind him to Gwen, who sat stiff on the edge of the sofa. I didn't need to read minds to know I'd just walked into a battlefield.

Even Devon who was normally smiling was tight lipped. "Keira." He nodded his head and then looked over at Gwen.

"Hi Devon, Gwen." I mumbled slipping into the room and taking a seat on the other end of the sofa away from Gwen. They'd been talking about me. Talking about the real reason, Gwen and I had taken so many 'business' trips. He knew!

Devon's eyes, hard as flint peered over at me. "It's good

you're here. We were just discussing what's to be done."

I looked up to Mary's spirit and she nodded before turning her gaze to her two children. When I looked at Gwen and Sean, my mouth fell open. I knew that Gwen had never seen Mary's spirit but Sean? From the way he stood, his hands in his pockets staring at his father, he didn't see his mother either.

"I'm going back to Toronto, to my job if they'll take me back." Sean's eyes never left his father's, and he was blocking me in his thoughts.

My heart fell at his words. But what had I really expected?

Finally Gwen spoke, "Dad knows everything, Keira. He knows about David Holmes, what you and I had been doing, the whole shebang." She snorted, "But you knew that already didn't you?" The disdain and sarcasm wafted from her body in dark waves.

Devon's voice was soft when he spoke, "I knew from the very start." When Mary's hand rose to rest on his shoulder, his head dipped to the side, a loving gesture between the two of them.

Of course. Devon knew Mary was there. He communicated with her. She'd told him everything. "It was Mary, wasn't it? I can see her nodding right now. She told you of my grandmother's work."

"What the hell? I hate that I'm the only one who can't see her!" Gwen blurted. "She's my mother and everyone but me can see her, talk to her?" Her jaw clenched and she shook her head sharply.

"Not everyone, Sis. I can't either which is really puzzling." Sean sighed and took a seat on the sofa between Gwen and me.

He was practically healed now, moving with the usual athletic grace and ease. He was so close to me, I could smell his aftershave, feel the heat of his body. A flash of the two of us that night in the hotel, laying and sleeping next to each other, appeared in my mind. His head turned sharply, and his eyes were wide looking at me.

Uh oh. I hadn't blocked him and he'd seen that same

image. My cheeks got warm and I looked away. Damn. Why did he have to be so damned good looking!

"So you can't see her either?" I asked him. It was a weak attempt to get back on track, to a more manageable mindset.

"You know I can't, Keira. I can see and sense everyone but her." He looked over at his father. "But you, Dad? You can see Mom? I didn't know that about you."

It was the first time that Devon smiled. "It's why I stay in this house. An apartment in the city would be easier but Mary wouldn't be there." He looked over at me, his eyes flaring. "And it's where she's gonna stay, you hear me? You can nudge any other spirit but her."

My hands flew up in front of me, "No problem." There was no way, I was upsetting him any more than I'd already done. His kids had been in serious trouble because of me.

Sean looked over at me and sighed. "You got that right. And Dad wants Gwen to continue with it."

"Your mother says its important work. I trust her." Devon turned to Gwen, "You know where I stand on this. It's not saying I won't worry, but some things are worth the risk. This is one of them."

"No Dad. It's not. I was kidnapped and Sean almost died. For what? So that spirits who are too messed up to pass through The Veil, will finally move on? No." She looked over at me and her eyes narrowed. "You're on your own, Keira."

It was the confirmation of what I'd dreaded. I looked over at Sean, but he was totally on-side with his sister. Hard to believe that Devon and I were the only ones devoted to this. But probably he wouldn't be either, if not for Mary.

I had to give it one more try. "Gwen, It's not that simple. You know that. If what we do, transitioning spirits to maintain order and the integrity of The Veil...if it wasn't important why would David Holmes have tried to stop us?" I stood up, looking down at Sean and her. "I hate what happened. But this work must continue. Even your parents—"

"Stop." Sean stood up, and his had gripped my shoulder. The breath caught in my throat. It was still there, the burst of energy exchange between us. "Gwen has heard enough from you, Keira." He stepped over to the archway and jerked his head to the side, "It's time for you to leave. Now."

I was numb as I crossed the room, Devon's protests for me to stay falling on deaf ears. When I passed by Sean, his words were hard, "And take your money with you. Not everyone has a price tag." His hand gripped my arm, "I might have liked you more, respected you even, if you hadn't tried to buy me."

My eyes flashed at him, "I wasn't doing that, Sean. I wanted you to have the freedom to do what it is you were destined for. It's certainly not pushing paper with Customs officials!"

"Destiny? You don't know anything about that. It's about choices. And right now, we don't choose to blindly follow you. I'm going back to my old life, to friends and a job pushing paper. I'll enjoy every boring minute." He yanked the door open and gestured with a sweep of his hand for me to leave.

In the nick of time, I held my tongue from blurting, 'coward'. He wasn't that certainly. Not after bursting into Holmes house and taking a bullet to save us. I scurried out the door and down the steps to my car before the wave of tears burst through. I was definitely on my own again.

FORTY

A couple of days later I sat at my laptop reading the latest email from Mr. Thompson.

Keira,

I've been contacted about an estate in Australia. Although the property has been vacant for over a decade, it was purchased by a charity with a view to creating a youth home for run-away teenagers. The problems first became known when several workmen, doing renovations to bring it up to speed have been hurt in mysterious accidents. They are on their third employee for night security and he is threatening to quit.

If you are interested in assisting them, please let me know. If something cannot be done soon, they will have to relinquish the project, losing money that they can hardly spare.

MICHELLE DOREY

Yours truly,
Charles Thompson

I read the email over again, sipping my second coffee in the sun room. It did sound like a classic haunting. And Australia? I'd always wanted to visit and see the beaches there. But, I was on my own. If nothing else, I'd have to hire someone to help me, in case it got too rough. At least someone would be able to call an ambulance.

Maybe I should take out an ad. *Wanted. Strong bodyguard with awesome psychic skills. No experience necessary. Will train.'* Yeah. Like that would ever happen. I'd have every kook in the world calling.

The door bell rang and I pushed myself up from the chair. Hell, I hadn't even hired a full time cook or housekeeper. Good luck with Guardian. When it rang again, I called out, "I'm coming! Hold your hat, will ya?" I walked quickly across the foyer and pulled the door open wide.

My mouth fell open, experiencing the strongest sense of deja vu I'd ever had. It was Gwen. But this time rather than carrying a mailbag, there was a suitcase in her hand. "Gwen? Hi!"

Her shoulders slumped a little and there was a scowl on her face. "He kicked me out. Can you believe that? After all I've done for him?"

My mouth opened and closed a few times before, I blurted. "What? Your Dad? He kicked you out?" Was this the same Devon who was the sweetest guy ever, kicking his only daughter out? Worlds collided. "Come in!" I grabbed the suitcase from her hand and stepped back inside.

"We had a huge fight. I told him I had contacted the post office to get my old job back and he totally lost it." Gwen's hair hung in lank curls over her shoulders and from the redness rimming her eyes, she'd been crying.

"Come on. I'll grab a coffee for you and you can tell me all about it." It was hard to keep my voice steady, when all I wanted to do was hoot for joy. Not that I liked that it had been a battle royal between them, but it might mean...

184

No. Don't jinx it.

I set the bag down and led the way to the kitchen. "I can't believe your father would do that." The irony of it. I'd ended up in this house after getting the boot from my parents, and now Gwen? But I wasn't in Gwen's league at all when it came to acting responsibly.

"Well he did! He said he was tired of seeing me throw my life away, nursing him. And delivering mail wasn't what I was destined to do."

Hmmm. He'd used my words, the ones I'd hurled at Sean. I got the mug down and poured coffee for her. "He's right. You have a gift Gwen. We were good together before...well before, you know."

She huffed a sigh and took the steaming mug from my hand. "Yeah...well, I guess."

She was already tripping down memory lane to the hauntings we'd worked on. She was almost there...

"And that's another thing! Stop with the Vulcan mind probe thingy. You're driving me nuts!"

I grinned. "You didn't mind it when you were in Holmes's clutches, if I recall." I took a seat at the small table and turned my laptop around for her to see.

But she was stubborn, purposely avoiding looking at it. "That was different." She sniffed and took a long sip of coffee.

"I promise, I won't invade your mind. Not if you don't want me to. Actually I learned a trick that I could teach you to prevent that." There was no way I was going to let her know that Jody had taught me the trick. Skating on pretty thin ice here...

Her eyes narrowed for a moment, "Okaaaay." She still didn't believe it was possible, but she'd see.

As nonchalantly as I could, "Did Sean go back to Toronto? What does he think?"

She leaned forward and this time the suspicion blazoned in her head, "Something happened between you two, didn't it? I mean, all that time you were together in that nightmare in the UK...He was really disappointed when you weren't there with me in the hospital. I think he likes you. And from the look on your face, it's mutual."

I could feel my cheeks getting warmer and warmer. Sean had a nice side that I liked. And I couldn't deny that I was attracted as hell to him. If only he hadn't turned back into asshat Sean. But I had to get by that. "How's Roy? Have you heard from him?"

"He's good. We're going to dinner tomorrow night. Why don't you come along?" Her smile was genuine and her eyes had taken on a sparkle just at the mention of his name.

And something inside me melted too. She was actually thinking of me, not leaving me out. "Maybe I will. Actually, I was thinking...we might need him around more. After that thing with David Holmes, it wouldn't hurt to have a guy watching our back."

She looked sheepish. "That didn't work out so good the last time. We were still kidnapped."

I took a deep breath and my jaw clenched. "But now we know about him. We'll be prepared. I think Roy could do it." I pushed the laptop closer to her. "Want to go to Australia with me?"

THE END

AUTHOR'S NOTE

I have been having a great time writing about Keira and Gwen (and now Roy and Sean...). I'm enjoying this series a great deal, and yes, there are other adventures ahead.

Thank you for reading this book, I truly hope you enjoyed it. Many, many hours went into its creation. Not only by myself, but also on the part of those near and dear to me. If you enjoyed it, please leave a review for it on Amazon. Honest reviews from readers such as yourself help authors, yes; but more importantly, your voice helps other readers a great deal in making their decisions.

ABOUT MICHELLE DOREY

A lifelong resident of Kingston, Michelle has experienced firsthand, eerie events. She's witnessed episodes where the veil between our world and the next has shimmered gossamer thin. These encounters fascinate rather than frighten her. On the other hand, her two pugs Ruby and Sookie freak out enough for the three of them. The Irish part of her heritage, stories of banshees, druids and, yes, leprechauns are what started her down the road of writing about the paranormal.

In the summer she dreams about skiing, and in the winter wishes she lived in Cuba. Yes, she's contrary as hell, but never boring. She hopes you enjoy reading her work as much as she enjoys writing it. She is currently practicing her acceptance speech for the Nobel Prize in Literature just in case. LOL

OTHER WORKS BY THE AUTHOR

THE HAUNTINGS OF KINGSTON

Crawley House
The Haunted Inn
The Ghosts of Centre Street
The Haunting Of Larkspur Farm
The Ghosts of Hanson House

THE MYSTICAL VEIL

Legacy
Heritage